UNLIKELY JAPAN
AND OTHER PLAYS

BY NEIL LABUTE

TEN ONE-ACT PLAYS
FROM TEN YEARS OF
THE LABUTE NEW THEATER FESTIVAL

Deplorable Play Publishing, Inc.
New York, NY

Praise for the LaBute New Theater Festival:

"LaBute has close ties to the St. Louis Actors' Studio, which since 2013 has produced an annual roster of one-acts, a form that LaBute has returned to again and again, to touch a wide range of raw nerves." — **Rollo Romig,** *The New Yorker*

"You hear lots of fresh voices, one right after another." —**Judith Newmark,** *St. Louis Post Dispatch*

"A rousing success. Patrons were treated to some well written and interpreted pieces that have validated the countless hours devoted by the festival's selection team to cull the best works from the hundreds of submissions they received." —**Mark Bretz,** *Ladue News*

"Mr. LaBute's writing is as skillful as ever." — **Elizabeth Vincentelli,** *The New York Times*

"Biting wit and hot-button drama." —**Lynn Venhaus,** *Limelight*

"St. Louis Actors' Studio delivers a knock out evening of new shows."
—**Tina Farmer,** *KDHX Radio*

"Mr. LaBute shows why he is the master with a beautifully crafted play."
—**Steve Allen,** *Stage Door St. Louis*

"A timely affirmation that LaBute remains among our most vital and necessary observers of messy modern life. That timeliness extends to the subject matter of the new plays." —**Elysa Gardner,** *New York Stage Review*

"An evening of essentially flawless live theater. Big ideas, clever scripts and top-notch performances across the board. Polished, professional and, most important, they each evoke an emotional response. That's why we go to the theater, and that's why the LaBute Fest matters." —**Paul Friswold,** *The Riverfront Times*

"When the lights go down on this one, you'll wish you had a few more minutes to think about the questions that are subtly posed within." —**Tanya Seale,** *Broadway World*

"The festival seems to gain steam every season." —**Andrea Torrence,** *St. Louis Theatre Snob*

Cast and Crew of The 2019 LaBute New Theater Festival, New York City

Neil LaBute on the Gaslight stage with the 2015 high school playwrights and cast members

Neil LaBute on the Gaslight stage with the 2013 playwrights

Copyright

This edition first published in the United States in 2024 by

Deplorable Play Publishing, Inc.
New York, NY

For bulk and special sales, please contact help@stlas.org.

Copyright© 2024 by Neil LaBute

NEIL LABUTE

Theatre includes: BASH: LATTER-DAY PLAYS (Douglas Fairbanks Theatre, Almeida Theatre); THE SHAPE OF THINGS (Almeida Theatre, Promenade Theatre); THE DISTANCE FROM HERE (MCC Theatre, Almeida Theatre); THE MERCY SEAT (MCC Theatre, Almeida Theatre); FILTHY TALK FOR TROUBLED TIMES (MCC Theatre); FAT PIG (MCC Theatre, Trafalgar Studios); AUTOBAHN (MCC Theatre); SOME GIRL(S) (Gielgud Theatre, MCC Theatre); THIS IS HOW IT GOES (Donmar Warehouse, The Public Theatre); LAND OF THE DEAD/HELTER SKELTER (Ensemble Studio Theatre, Bush Theatre); WRECKS (Everyman Palace Theatre, The Public Theatre, The Bush Theatre); IN A DARK DARK HOUSE (MCC Theatre, Almeida Theatre); THE BREAK OF NOON (MCC Theatre, Geffen Playhouse); REASONS TO BE PRETTY (MCC Theatre, Almeida Theatre); IN A FOREST, DARK AND DEEP (Vaudeville Theatre, Profiles Theatre); THE HEART OF THE MATTER (MCC Theatre); WOYZECK – adaptation (Schauspielhaus-Zurich); THINGS WE SAID TODAY (Profiles Theatre, Sala Beckett); THE FURIES/THE NEW TESTAMENT/ROMANCE (59E59); THE GREAT WAR (Ensemble Studio Theatre); TAMING OF THE SHREW - additional scenes (Chicago Shakespeare Theatre); SHORT ENDS (Open Fist Theatre); LOVELY HEAD (Spoleto Festival-Italy, Fringe Festival-Madrid, La Mama); IN THE BEGINNING (Edinburgh Fringe Festival, Theatre Row); MISS JULIE – adaptation (Geffen Playhouse); REASONS TO BE HAPPY (MCC Theatre, Hampstead Theatre); GOOD LUCK [In Farsi] (59E59); OVER THE RIVER AND THROUGH THE WOODS (Planet Connections Theatre Festivity); PICK ONE (Edinburgh Fringe Festival, Young Vic); ONE DAY LIKE THIS (American Academy of Dramatic Arts); HERE WE GO 'ROUND THE MULBERRY BUSH (St. Louis Actors' Studio); I'M GOING TO STOP PRETENDING THAT I DIDN'T BREAK YOUR HEART (Venice Biennale); THE MONEY SHOT (MCC Theatre); HAPPY HOUR (La Mama), EXHIBIT 'A' (Theatre Delicatessen); THE WAY WE GET BY (Second Stage); 10K (59E59); MOHAMMED GETS A BONER (Planet Connections

Theatre Festivity); KANDAHAR (St. Louis Actors' Studio); 16 POUNDS (Trafalgar Studios); ALL THE WAYS TO SAY I LOVE YOU (MCC Theatre); I DON'T KNOW WHAT I CAN SAVE YOU FROM (La Mama); BREAK POINT (59E59) WE HAVE A SITUATION (Konstanz Theatre – Germany); HATE CRIME (St. Louis Actors' Studio); REASONS TO BE PRETTY HAPPY (MCC Theatre); GREAT NEGRO WORKS OF ART and UNLIKELY JAPAN (St. Louis Actors' Studio), APPOMATTOX (59E59), COMFORT (St. Louis Actors' Studio), THE ANSWER TO EVERYTHING (Staatstheater - Augsberg), SEVEN DATES (Sala Beckett - Barcelona) and IT'S NOT YOU, IT'S ME (Radu Stancu National Theater - Sibiu).

Film includes: IN THE COMPANY OF MEN; YOUR FRIENDS & NEIGHBORS; NURSE BETTY; POSSESSION; THE SHAPE OF THINGS; THE WICKER MAN; LAKEVIEW TERRACE; DEATH AT A FUNERAL; SOME GIRL(S); SOME VELVET MORNING; DIRTY WEEKEND; OUT OF THE BLUE; FEAR THE NIGHT; HOUSE OF DARKNESS; TUMBLE (short); AFTER-SCHOOL SPECIAL (short); SEXTING (short); DENISE (short); DOUBLE OR NOTHING (short); BENCH SEAT (short); SWEET NOTHINGS (short); BFF (short); IT'S OKAY (short); GOOD LUCK [IN FARSI] (short); THE MULBERRY BUSH (short); 10K (short); OVER THE RIVER AND THROUGH THE WOODS (short); BLACK CHICKS (short) and SPARRING PARTNER (short).

Television includes: BASH: LATTER-DAY PLAYS (Showtime); FULL CIRCLE (Directv); TEN X TEN (Directv); BILLY & BILLIE (Directv); VAN HELSING (SYFY), THE I-LAND (Netflix) and the upcoming AUTOBAHN.

Fiction includes: SECONDS OF PLEASURE (Faber & Faber).

What a long strange trip it's been.

Jerry Garcia might have said it first—I doubt it—but it certainly applies to the journey that William Roth and I have taken over the last ten years or so, first as collaborators at his 'Actors' Studio of Saint Louis' and then as co-conspirators of the 'LaBute New Theater Festival' that has spawned ten years' worth of short plays, both in St. Louis and New York, from dozens of playwrights, both professionals and newcomers (plus high school students as well).

I'm proud to have been an active participant throughout this decade of creativity and to have watched William work tirelessly at creating a venue for new writing in the short form, which is a kind of playwriting I love and admire, as both a practitioner and an audience member. It is deceptively difficult to write short work, be it for the stage or the screen or the page—just ask any songwriter—and it can take a lifetime to fully conquer the form, if ever.

That said, writers have always been attracted to the challenge and some of the best stage plays that now exist are an hour or less. Without the one-act play we wouldn't have MISS JULIE or THE ZOO STORY or DUTCHMAN or TRIFLES or RIDERS TO THE SEA or SEVEN JEWISH CHILDREN and the list goes on and on. Some of my own best work for the theater has come in 30 pages or less and, hopefully, a few of those pieces were written for this very festival and are now contained within the pages of the volume you hold in your hands.

One of the many great things about the yearly festival that William continues to nurture is that each play picked by the selection committee gets a fully staged production at his home venue in Missouri and that is invaluable for any writer to witness. Theater work never fully comes to life until it is in the hands of a director and actors (and in front of a live audience) and no amount of staged readings can ever take the place of that electrifying experience. It is the moment that playwrights live for and the 'LaBute New Theater Festival' brings those hopes to fruition on a yearly basis; I'm very proud that the festival carries my name on it and that I get a chance to write a new play for it every summer. May the process continue for a long time to come.

The ten shorts contained in this volume are quite diverse, from comedy to drama, from dialogue to monologue, and all written with a passion for the actors who would go on to breathe life into the many characters on display. Thank you to all of the performers, directors and crew members who helped these ideas spring to life at the Gaslight Theatre (and a few different venues in New York City as well).

In subsequent printings we hope to publish many more short plays by a variety of our participating authors but for our inaugural volume we felt that my work over the course of the past decade would well represent our collective efforts.

I hope you enjoy these ten one-acts and may they even arouse a creative impulse in you that leads to a short play of your own; it's never too late to become an author.

Until it is.

Neil LaBute
April 2024

Festival staff

- **Neil LaBute** – Film Director, Screenwriter and Playwright

- **William Roth** – Founder, Artistic Director St. Louis Actors' Studio

- **John Pierson** – Assoc. Artistic Director

- **Annamaria Pileggi** – Assoc. Artistic Director

- **Patrick Huber** – Assoc. Artistic Director - Set Design and Lighting Design

- **Amy Paige** – Resident Stage Manager

- **Lizi Watt** – Submissions Lead

- **Kristi Gunther** – Production Manager

- **Jenny Smith, Lisa Beke** – Prop Design

- **Carla Landis Evans, Teresa Doggett, Abby Pastorello** – Costume Design

- **Joe Novak, Caleb Long** – Set Construction

- **Jonathan Zelezniak** – TD, Light Design, Set Construction NYC

Special Thanks

Milton Zoth, Michael Hogan, Nathan Bush, Julie Schoettley, Edward Scott Ibur, Elizabeth Helman, Maggie Doyle Ervin, Carol Cordani, Wendy Renee Greenwood, Spencer Sickmann, Eric Dean White, Bryn McLaughlin, Kelly Robertson, Kristopher Robertson, Gia Crovatin, Clea Alsip, Keilyn Durrel Jones, Brenda Meaney, Liz Masucci, Josephine Roth and Elisa Roth

TABLE OF CONTENTS

THE POSSIBLE

THE POSSIBLE had its world premiere at the Gaslight Theater as part of the 'LaBute New Theater Festival' in St. Louis Missouri in July 2013. It was directed by Milton Zoth.

One: Rachel Shin (Fenton)
Two: Wendy Renee Greenwood

A slash (/) indicates where the next actor should speak.

(left to right) Wendy Renee Greenwood, Rachel Shin (Fenton)
Photo: STLAS

TWO WOMEN ARE SITTING IN A LIVING ROOM. STARING AT EACH OTHER.

ONE ...so.

TWO ...

ONE Lemme understand this...

TWO Sure.

ONE Because it's a little bit...you know...

TWO I know.

ONE It's not what I expected you to say.

TWO I know it's not.

ONE I came here ready to be all...whatever. To yell at you...to confront you...

TWO I get that. I understand. But...

ONE But now you're...I don't even know what to think about this. What you just said.

TWO Think what you want. It's the truth.

ONE You're... (BEAT) No. It's not possible.

TWO You sure about that? You sure?

ONE I mean...that's...but why would you do that? Seriously, why?

TWO Exactly why I said...

ONE ...yeah, but...if you really wanted to...

TWO I'm not making shit up, okay? I'm not trying to get out of this, saying 'you don't know what you're talking about...you're crazy if you think I'd ever try to sleep with your boyfriend'...I'm not saying that. At all. (BEAT) Am I?

ONE ...no...

TWO Alright then. So?

ONE   So...you...went after my boyfriend, like, aggressively after him for the last month or so...just so you could...then...what?

TWO   You know.

ONE   ...no...

TWO   You know exactly why. Yes, you do.

ONE   For *me*?

TWO   That's right.

ONE   To get me. To be with me.

TWO   Yes. I slept with your boyfriend so I could be with you...so that I would eventually end up with you.

ONE   That's...no! NO!! That's ridiculous!

TWO   Still...that was the plan. (BEAT) And here you are, by the way.

ONE   No! I'm here to yell at you, to tell you to 'fuck off!' and stay out of our lives, that's why I'm here!!! Not for any other reason!!!

TWO   We'll see...

ONE   I am!! I'm here for that!!

TWO   And where's your boyfriend?

ONE   He's at work...he's...it doesn't matter!

TWO   Does he know you're here?

ONE   ...

TWO   Does he?

ONE   No...I didn't...I found out about this and I...I mean, I confronted him and he denied it...said It never happened...

TWO   But that's not true. Is it?

ONE I'm...

TWO Is-it?

ONE I don't know now. (BEAT) I don't know.

TWO What's that mean?

ONE It means he says he didn't do anything...that he barely knows you and would never hurt me or do that kind of thing to me, but then I come to you and you say the opposite...you say it did happen. (BEAT) Several times.

TWO That's right.

ONE So...I'm...I'm...I'm...

TWO But no, that's...I didn't just say it...did I? That's not completely true.

ONE No.

TWO No...I did more than that. I showed you that it happened...I gave you evidence that it did.

ONE Yes.

TWO E-mails.

ONE Yes.

TWO And texts.

ONE Yes.

TWO Quite a few texts.

ONE Yes. That's...

TWO And more, too...didn't I? More than that.

ONE Yes.

TWO Just a few minutes ago. Right there... (POINTING) On the coffee table.

ONE I guess you did. Yes.

WOMAN TWO POINTS AT A SMALL STACK OF PAPERS ON A TABLE NEARBY. OFFERS ONE OR TWO OF THEM UP AGAIN.

TWO   A hotel receipt. A hotel that I paid for but that he signed a room service ticket for at least twice...two different meals that we ate after having sex...

ONE   Ok. Alright. Yes. (BEAT) Fine.

TWO   So yeah...I think I did a little bit more than just 'say' it happened.

WOMAN ONE DOESN'T KNOW HOW TO RESPOND. WOMAN TWO SLIDES DOWN TO HER AND GETS CLOSE. A HAND ON HER KNEE. WOMAN ONE PULLS AWAY.

ONE   But...you're...

TWO   What?

ONE   I dunno! It doesn't even make sense! None of this makes any sense at all...

TWO   It does to me...

ONE   How? How does doing that...with him...make any sense if what you want-- if you really do honestly want to be with me--how is this a normal way of going about that? I, I, I, I, I don't understand.

TWO   Because you're with him. I needed to get you away from him. (BEAT) Simple.

ONE   But then why would I ever want to be with you...the person who ruined that? Hmmmmm?

TWO   True. (BEAT) That part was a risk...

ONE   I don't even like women! I mean, as...you know...in relationships, I'm say- ing.

TWO   That can change. (BEAT) It can.

ONE   Yeah, no offense, but...I doubt it.

TWO   'Doubt' is not 'no.' 'Doubt' is not even close to 'no.'

ONE   Then 'no.' I'm not a lesbian...I am not interested. There. (BEAT) NO.

TWO   I'm not signing people up today, so don't worry about it. This isn't a rally.

ONE   This is so frustrating! I mean...God!!

TWO   All I care about is you...you being with me...I'm not here to convert you. (BEAT) We can 'call' it whatever you want...

ONE   I don't want to have sex with a woman! Shit, do you not understand what I just said to you...

TWO   And..have you ever done that?

ONE   What?

TWO   Had sex. With a woman.

WOMAN ONE PAUSES FOR A BEAT. THINKING. SHE FINALLY SAYS:

ONE   No.

TWO   Never?

ONE   No! (BEAT) I mean...

TWO   What?

ONE   Just...stop! Stop it! I'm really fucking angry at you right now, ok, so just...

TWO   That doesn't mean you can't answer that. It's just a question.

ONE   Once. In college. One time I...there was a girl in my dorm...she came on to me a few times.

TWO   A few?

ONE   Yes! A few. Over the course of a semester or, or...however long...

TWO   I see.

ONE   But we never did anything!

TWO   No?

ONE   No. I always...I stopped her. Before.

TWO Ok.

ONE Alright?

TWO Fine by me. (BEAT) Right before or, like, at the door? (BEAT) I'm just wondering...how long did you let her go before putting up a fight?

ONE STOP!

TWO I'm just asking...

ONE We never even kissed. Not once. So...

TWO So then how do you know?

ONE Know what?

TWO That you're not one.

ONE I'm not! I'm just not...I like men. I like...that. I'm straight or, you know, whatever you'd call that. I'm sure you guys've got a name for it...

TWO Who? Which 'guys?'

ONE You guys! Lesbians. Lesbian women.

TWO I'm not a lesbian...

ONE Oh really? No? You're not?

TWO Nope.

ONE Okay, you know what...this is too...

TWO If I'm anything I'm Bi but I don't get into 'labels' all that much...I hate to be seen as just one thing. Something you can stick a post-it on, so no...I don't really think of myself as anything but just 'me.'

ONE Fine.

TWO Fine or not, that's just who I am.

ONE Great, so, you go be the...super liberal bi-girl or whatever you are and I'm just gonna...I'll...just...

TWO What?

A MOMENTARY PAUSE UNTIL WOMAN ONE JUMPS UP AND SHOUTS:

ONE I'm going! I'm leaving now and I want you to stay the fuck away from my boyfriend!

TWO Got it. Ok. I got it.

ONE Yeah?! Well...I hope so!

WOMAN ONE STANDS THERE WAITING BUT WOMAN TWO DOES NOT ENGAGE WITH HER. FINALLY SHE SAYS:

TWO You can leave any time you want to...

WOMAN ONE IS THINKING, TRYING TO DECIDE HER NEXT MOVE.

ONE No! That's not...no!! You know what?! I'm not leaving until you apologize for...for all the shit you've done to me! To us!!

TWO 'I apologize.' (SMILES) Better?

ONE ...no.

TWO Then what else do you want me to say? 'I won't do it again?' Something like that?

ONE I mean...yes! You won't...will you?

TWO I don't know yet.

ONE What does that mean?

TWO If I think it might help me...then yes.

ONE Help you what?

TWO Don't be coy.

ONE Just...stop, okay? Stop-that. (BEAT) I am not into women...I don't want that in my life...I don't want 'you.' Alright? Is it clear enough if I say it that way? (BEAT) Not interested. Not attracted. Not going to go there. WITH YOU.

TWO   Maybe so.

ONE   Oh my God!

TWO   The thing is...you just said the exact same stuff your boyfriend said to me, first time we met up for coffee. (BEAT) Mind you, he didn't have to meet me... I called him, asked him to but he had absolutely no actual reason to do it. He spent the whole first evening telling me about all the reasons that we couldn't be together, every great thing about you and what he wanted to happen for you guys in the next couple years. All that crap. He said it to my face...he slapped his hand down on the table a few times. Everything you should do when you're in a relationship with a person. He did it all. (BEAT) Then I paid the check and he walked me home--again, didn't need to but he did--came up for a drink and then he fucked my brains out. A few times. (BEAT) Next visit or two he didn't say very much at all...in fact, nothing about you.

ONE   Please don't tell me all this...

TWO   I'm not doing it to hurt you. I'm just saying...as a fact...that because you look at me right now and tell me that there's no chance for the two of us...but you're still standing here while you say it, instead of throwing that drink in my face and shouting it at me from down the stairs...I somehow feel like I've still got a shot here. So forgive my apparent confidence but I need to go with my gut on this one...

WOMAN ONE STANDS AND STARTS TO GATHER HER THINGS. COAT AND PURSE AND STUFF LIKE THAT.

ONE   Then I'll go. I'll get out of here...I'll take my stuff and just...go home.

TWO   Alright. It was nice to see you.

ONE   That's... (TURNS TO HER) Why me? I just don't even...out of all the people out there...people who would find you great and attractive and, and, and...why would you pick someone like me? (BEAT) Huh?

TWO   You think I'm attractive?

ONE   Agghhhh! You know what I mean! WHY?!

TWO Of course I know...but I'm interested in the other thing you just said...

ONE God, you know what? Forget it...

TWO No, come on. Just answer that. Answer it and I'll stop bugging you. I promise.

ONE What? (STOPS) Answer what?

TWO Do you find me attractive? At all?

ONE That's...not...who cares?! WHO FUCKING CARES RIGHT NOW?!!

TWO I do. I care. (BEAT) Isn't that obvious?

ONE You're...yes, obviously. You are a very pretty...whatever. A beautiful girl or, you know...I don't know! It doesn't at all matter what I think! (BEAT) You did an awful thing to me...to my boyfriend and me...and I'll never forgive you for that! Ever! So it doesn't really matter if I think you're good-looking or not...I could never be with you now so what do your care if I like your face?!!

TWO Well...

ONE What? (BEAT) *What?*

TWO I just...people can forgive so much in life...like, I mean, really horrific stuff sometimes...things like rape or, you know, the Holocaust and shit like that...growing up Catholic...I do feel like it's possible...

ONE What is? Me forgiving you?

TWO I do, yeah. I think you could. Given enough time I do think so...

ONE Well, I don't want to...so...

TWO No, ok, maybe so, but that's different. I'm just saying...I think you could. If the right circumstances came along...if you realized that I'd actually done you a big favor...then yeah...maybe you could.

ONE A 'favor?' You think what you've done for me is a favor? Trying to split me up from a guy I really care about? That's a good thing?

TWO   I think so, yeah...

ONE   Really? You do?

TWO   Yep...and so will you. In time. I really do believe that.

WOMAN TWO LOOKS AT THE OTHER WOMAN FOR A BEAT, THEN SAYS:

TWO   ...are you gonna marry him? This guy of yours?

ONE   What?!

TWO   I'm just asking...

ONE   That's none of your business!

TWO   I didn't say it was...I just asked if you were going to...

ONE   Maybe! Yeah, yeah...maybe I will...

TWO   Which means...

ONE   Which means 'maybe!' (BEAT) We've talked about it, yes we have, but I don't know when or what month, anything like that...

TWO   Even with what you know about him and me now? About what we've done?

ONE   I don't know! I-DON'T-KNOW! STOP IT!

TWO   You know what? Maybe you were right...you should go now because you're not ready to talk about this. It's too raw right now.

WOMAN TWO WALKS AWAY, LEAVING WOMAN ONE TO STARE AT HER FROM BEHIND. SHE FINALLY SAYS:

ONE   Oh, ok, now you don't wanna talk about it because I yelled at you...

TWO   No, I don't mind that. I kinda liked it, actually...gave me the chills...

ONE   Stop doing that! Stop talking to me like that!

TWO   How? How am I talking to you?

ONE   You know! You know what you're doing...in a slinky sort of way...with that sound in your voice and, and...these insinuations and this kind of...I don't know what it is but I do know what you're doing!

TWO   Yeah? What's that?

ONE   You're seducing me! That's what you are trying to do...you're seducing me! (BEAT) Aren't you?

TWO   Am I?

ONE   See?!

TWO   What?

ONE   Every question...you say another one...you answer all my questions with another question...

TWO   Do I?

ONE   YES!

TWO   So?

ONE   Just like that!

TWO   Like what?

ONE   Please...stop it...

TWO   Why? Why should I stop? Do you want me to stop? I mean, really?

ONE   Yes.

TWO   You do?

ONE   Yes. I do.

TWO   Are you sure? I mean, one-hundred percent sure?

ONE   ...

WOMAN ONE GIVES UP FOR A MOMENT. WOMAN TWO NOTICES THIS.

TWO See?

ONE What?

TWO That was 'silence.' That wasn't 'I'm one hundred-percent-sure.'

ONE No...that's...no. I'm just confused.

TWO Really? Why?

ONE Because I came here to...to...

TWO I know, I know, you came here to chastise me...to say what an awful person I am...

ONE ...yes...I mean, sort of...yes.

TWO And you've done that now. So?

ONE Yeah, but...I don't even think you care.

TWO Does that matter?

ONE I mean...it's always better if what you say to someone has an impact...that it means something...

TWO And it did. I heard you.

ONE Ok.

TWO I'm not saying it's going to change me...make me live my life differently, but...

ONE But you did hear me, right? Correct?

TWO Yes. I heard you. Loud and clear.

ONE Alright. (BEAT) Then...

TWO And me? Did you hear what I had to say to you?

ONE About what...?

TWO You. Your boyfriend. Who you are.

ONE I mean...

TWO How many boyfriends have you had in the last...say...ten years? Since you started dating, even.

ONE I'm...look, I need to get home...

TWO Why? You can't even answer a question for me now? One question?

ONE Fine! I'm not sure...actual boyfriends? Or just...?

TWO Yes. Slept with. Loved. Thought about in a long-term kind of arrangement way. That sort of guy.

ONE Maybe...like...five.

TWO ...

ONE Seven. Or so.

TWO And how many of those ended?

ONE What?

TWO 'Ended?' Like finished...at some point?

ONE Ummmmmmmmmm...

TWO I mean, *all*, right? All of your relationships ended...even this one, that you're in now...look what he's done. With me.

ONE So?

TWO So I'm saying it's going to end.

ONE No! No, it's not...

TWO Yes, it is. Maybe not because of this...maybe it'll take until after you marry and have kids...but it's going to end.

ONE You don't know that! (BEAT) You don't.

TWO I promise it will. I-PROMISE.

ONE   That's...and so what? What if it does? What the hell does that prove?

TWO   Something. About you.

ONE   That's not even...what're you saying? If a person can't find happiness with someone of the opposite sex then they're...?

TWO   Maybe.

ONE   That's ridiculous! That is so...come on! That's just...whatever. Ridiculous.

TWO   Is it?

ONE   Yes! I mean...what? Liz Taylor? Lesbian? Cary Grant? Gay? (BEAT) Okay, that might be a bad example...but...

TWO   It's possible, that's what I'm saying. All I care about is the possible...

ONE   If people don't stay in one relationship or...or find the right person... then that person is gay? Is that what you're trying to tell me here? I mean...

TWO   I'm saying it's possible. I'm saying that it's highly possible--probable, even--the person we're talking about should take a really good, long look at themselves and see if they are who they think they are.

ONE   You're just one of those people who take things...you want what you want when you want it and if you don't get it you ruin people. Families. Lives. You ruin stuff when you're not happy or can't have what you want or think you want! (BEAT) You want me. I say you can't have that and so you're willing to rub my nose in the fact that my boyfriend is weak, he's a shit, and like thousands of other guys who would sleep with a beautiful woman if given a chance. So what? SO-WHAT? I probably already knew that about him...I mean, of course I did...he's a guy...of course I did! Thank you for showing me exactly what I already feared and I already knew about men in general and my partner in particular! THANK YOU SO VERY MUCH!!

WOMAN TWO GOES TO HER AND TURNS HER AROUND. FACE TO FACE.

TWO   So prove it then...

ONE   What?

TWO   Prove that you're not what I say you are. That you're not what I want you to be...that you aren't the person I've been looking for all of my life.

ONE   ...

TWO   Because I think you are...I thought that the minute I saw you at that party last summer. You know what I'm talking about. The party. In the summer. You were there with you-know-who and I was there with you-don't-know-her--or want to know her, frankly--and we met going in and out of the house...I was going in to use their bathroom, you were just coming out...we passed in the doorway...at the very same moment...

ONE   ...the French doors...

TWO   Yes. Those. (SMILES) You remember.

ONE   Yeah...we passed each other. We smiled.

TWO   Exactly.

ONE   We, we looked at each other and we...so what?

TWO   You know what.

ONE   No, I honestly don't. No.

TWO   That's not true! You're not being honest!

ONE   I am too!! I did not feel anything!! Not anything for you, anyway! It's not true!

TWO   I don't believe you.

ONE   Why?!

TWO   Because it hit me like a thunderbolt. I'm a woman who has done a lot in my relatively short little lifetime...been with many people...seen many things... traveled the world a bit...and nothing has stopped me in my tracks like that smile from you. That tiny glance you gave me. Time froze. My life changed. Everything I've ever wanted or felt or needed--and I don't use a word like that one very often, *need*--all of it changed the moment, the very second, in fact, I met you...

saw you. Became aware of your existence in this cold, crazy, terribly arbitrary but yes...occasionally beautiful world of ours...

ONE   ...stop...please...

TWO   I think you could be everything to me...all that I can ever imagine in my life. I have to have you. HAVE-TO. (BEAT) Just so you know...

ONE   I'm...not...

TWO   I don't care what you're not. I want you to find out what you are. Who you are.

ONE   You'll never know who I am...not ever. You can't. I won't let you.

TWO   Yes, you will.

ONE   No, I won't. NO.

TWO   I already do./ I know you.

ONE   No.../ No, you don't.

TWO   Yes, I do./ I do, too.

ONE   No, you don't!/ YOU DON'T!

TWO   Of course I do.../ YES, I DO!

ONE   You can't!/ You can't know me...who I am or what I want!! You're just saying what you want, that's all!! This is what YOU want!!/ It's all about YOU!!!

TWO   Of course it is./ I want you, yes, I do! I want you! I WANT YOU! I WANT YOU! Have you ever really been wanted...wanted the way I want you?!/ No, I don't think so!!

ONE   That's.../ I don't know...

TWO   You never have and you never will! NEVER, NEVER, NEVER! DON'T YOU UNDERSTAND THAT?!

ONE   ...

TWO   This is it. This is everything…

WOMAN ONE HAS NOTHING TO SAY IN RETURN. WOMAN TWO SPEAKS:

TWO   One time.

ONE   What?

TWO   Kiss me one time. Touch me once. My face, my arm, my shoulder. Some part of me. Do that. Tell me you don't feel what I do…say that and I'll never bother you again. I will disappear from your life. Promise. (BEAT) I *promise*.

ONE   That's…what'll that prove?

TWO   That anything's possible. Anything.

ONE   …

WOMAN TWO MOVES CLOSER TO WOMAN ONE. ONLY INCHES APART.

TWO   Dare you. (BEAT) I-dare-you.

ONE   Once…?

TWO   Just once. (BEAT) Just one time…

WOMAN ONE DOESN'T MOVE. WOMAN TWO MOVES TO HER. KISSES HER. SLOWLY AT FIRST BUT IT BUILDS. FINALLY THEY BOTH PULL AWAY. LOOKING AT EACH OTHER.

TWO   …and?

WOMAN ONE STARES LONG AND HARD INTO THE EYES OF WOMAN TWO BEFORE SHE SOFTLY SAYS:

ONE   …gimme a minute…

WOMAN TWO SMILES AT THIS. WOMAN ONE MOVES CLOSER TO WOMAN TWO AND THEY KISS AGAIN. DOESN'T LOOK LIKE THIS WILL END ANY TIME SOON.

HERE WE GO 'ROUND THE MULBERRY BUSH

HERE WE GO 'ROUND THE MULBERRY BUSH had its world premiere at the Gaslight Theater as part of the 'LaBute New Theater Festival' in St. Louis Missouri in July 2014. It was directed by Milton Zoth.

Kip: Reginald Pierre
Bill: William Roth

(left to right) Reginald Pierre, William Roth
Photo: Patrick Huber

A STRETCH OF GRASS AND FLOWER BEDS. BENCHES AS WELL. SOME CORNER OF A PARK SOMEWHERE. THE SOUND OF CHILDREN PLAYING IN THE DIS-TANCE. A MAN IN HIS 50S SITTING ON ONE OF THE BENCHES. HE HAS A PAPER WITH HIM BUT HE'S NOT READING IT. THIS IS 'BILL.' HE JUST SITS AND STARES. CHECKS HIS WATCH FROM TIME TO TIME. TAKES A BITE FROM AN UNWRAPPED SANDWICH. AFTER A MOMENT ANOTHER MAN ENTERS. SITS ON A BENCH NEAR BILL. HE'S MID-30S. WORK CLOTHES. HIS NAME IS 'KIP.' BILL GLANCES AT KIP. NODS. KIP RETURNS THE GESTURE. THEY SIT. THEY STARE.

KIP   ...beautiful day, huh?

BILL   Gorgeous.

KIP   Yeah. I know. (BEAT) Terrible winter we had, so...thank God. Right?

BILL   Uh-huh. So cold.

KIP   Yep. That was the thing...people saying it was one of the worst on record and all that, but to me it just seemed cold. The snow stuck around because of that...not like it just kept coming...piling up or anything...but really cold. So it stayed.

BILL   That's true.

KIP   Anyway... (POINTING) It's spring now. It feels great--last few weeks, month even--it's been fantastic.

BILL   I agree.

KIP   Yep. Baseball's back...

BILL   Right.

KIP   ...March Madness...

BILL   Oh yeah. (BEAT) And Mr. Softie!

KIP   Ha! Absolutely! Love that.

BILL   Me, too! That's when it's official, far as I'm concerned. I see those trucks and it's pretty much clear sailing from there on in...

KIP   Uh-huh.

BILL   Summer is right around the corner.

KIP   That's true...

BILL   Kids all lined up there, waiting for that soft-serve. (BEAT) You know?

KIP   Yep! And me right behind 'em...waiting to push 'em outta the way if I have to! I'm kidding, but...you know. (BEAT) I love to get a cone this time of year. Chocolate.

BILL   Not me.

KIP   No?

BILL   Nope. Old-fashioned vanilla, thank you very much... (BEAT) Simple and classic.

KIP   Hmmmmm. 'Sprinkles?'

BILL   Sure. Well, I'm old enough to call them 'jimmies' but same thing. (GRINS) I love those. (GRINS) Yummy.

KIP   Wait...what? Which is which? Are they the same thing, 'sprinkles' and 'jimmies?'

BILL   Ummmmmm...I think so... (BEAT) No?

KIP   I dunno...I'm asking.

BILL   I think--am I wrong about that?

KIP   Maybe. I always thought that--aren't just the chocolate ones called 'jimmies?'

BILL   Oh. Are they?

KIP   Pretty sure. (BEAT) Wait...

BILL   They're not just 'chocolate sprinkles?'

KIP   ...

BILL   Or 'jimmies?' I think they're one in the same. 'Jimmies' and 'sprinkles.'

KIP No, I'm pretty sure--not sure-sure, but you know--that the chocolate ones are the ones you call 'jimmies.' (BEAT) I dunno!

BILL Yeah?

KIP I think.

BILL And the other ones are what?

KIP Just sprinkles. Or maybe they're called 'rainbow sprinkles.' Maybe that's it...

BILL Huh. (BEAT) Okay. (BEAT) Well, I'll ask next time...

KIP Sounds good.

THE TWO MEN SMILE AT THIS AND NOD. BILL LOOKS DOWN AT HIS WRIST-WATCH. KIP NOTICES THIS, ALONG WITH SOME TOYS ON BILL'S BENCH.

BILL Either way...I love that. A beautiful day and an ice cream. With the what-ever-you-call-ems on it. Sprinkled on there...and you come over here and sit. In the park. (BEAT) That's lovely.

KIP Sounds great.

BILL Trust me. (SMILES) It's perfect.

KIP Yeah?

BILL Oh yes. This is such a nice spot.

KIP Yeah?

BILL Mmmmmmm. On a day like this? Wonderful. (BEAT) I'll sit here for hours when I'm not working. Taking in the sun.

KIP I'll bet.

BILL Quiet, you know? More so than the rest of the park. Down by the ball fields. Other places like that. And gorgeous light...

KIP Right.

BILL A bit more secluded.

KIP Yeah, I can see that...

BILL You can read, or...you know...have your lunch. (INDICATES) A sandwich.

KIP Uh-huh. (BEAT) Yeah, it's tucked back in here a ways. Off the path. That's nice. (WAITS) Listen to those kids...

BILL I know.

KIP So happy to be outta the house...makes you smile to hear 'em out there, laughing and playing. Doesn't it?

BILL Yes. Sounds like they're having fun.

KIP Totally. (BEAT) That doesn't bother you?

BILL Excuse me?

KIP No, I just mean...when you were saying it stays quieter over here--this end of the park--that doesn't bug you? The kids? If you're reading your paper or whatever...eating your egg salad there?

BILL No. Not at all.

KIP Well, that's good...

BILL Yes, they're fine. (POINTING) They're way over there. Down by the--pretty far away.

KIP Oh. Right. Yeah, I see...by that little gate. (BEAT) Some probably come up this way, though, right? A few? Don't they?

BILL Sometimes. Not too often.

KIP No? (BEAT) Huh.

BILL No, they're not much of a bother. (BEAT) They just like to explore and that sort of thing. Bring their dogs up here...

KIP Nice. (BEAT) You got any?

BILL Animals?

KIP   No! The other kind…

BILL   Hmmmm?

KIP   Kids. Do you have children?

BILL   Oh! Sorry! (LAUGHS) I don't. No. None of my own…

KIP   Got it.

BILL   Wasn't lucky enough for that to happen in my life…so…

KIP   Huh. But you'd like some? Or one, even? I mean…if you could?

BILL   Ummmmmm…

KIP   You don't have to answer that! Sorry.

BILL   That's alright.

KIP   None of my business, really…

BILL   It's fine.

KIP   I mean…not 'none' but you don't have to say anything. (BEAT) If you don't wanna.

BILL   Hmmmm? (CHECKS HIS WATCH) What's that?

KIP   …

BILL   I didn't follow you…

KIP   …

BILL   You said something…I missed the part about…did you say that it was or was not your business? My having children? (BEAT) Sorry?

KIP   Ummmmmmmmm…neither. I said it was sort 'of somewhere in-between, I guess.

BILL   I'm not…I'm afraid I'm lost…what?

KIP   In-between.

BILL What does that mean?

KIP I mean...yes...you're right...it's not really my 'business' if you have a kid or not, that's not what I'm--but I have a kid, and you know him. And that is my business. (BEAT) That part. (BEAT) They won't be coming here today, by the way. My wife. My kid. (BEAT) Today it's just gonna be us. (BEAT) You and me. (BEAT) So you can quit checking your watch...

BILL ...

KIP (LOOKING OVER) Well, that made you quiet.

BILL No...not at all...I just don't...

KIP What? (BEAT) Don't know what to say...or which one I'm talking about? Which kid?

BILL I don't...I'm not sure I like your tone. Mr...?

KIP Simms. My name is 'Kip Simms.' Yours?

BILL I'm 'Bill.' (BEAT) My name's 'Bill.'

KIP Oh. (WAITS) 'Bill' what?

BILL 'Bill Jensen.'

KIP 'Bill Jensen.' (BEAT) Yeah, you're him. I got the right guy. (BEAT) I suppose there was always the chance that I could've sat down next to someone else... different guy who accidentally sat where you usually do in the afternoons...that is possible.

BILL Listen...Mr. Simms...I'm not sure...

KIP 'Kip' really is fine, you can just call me that. 'Kip.' I prefer it. (BEAT) Kip.

BILL Fine, 'Kip'...

KIP No need to get formal or anything.

BILL ...alright...

KIP Not yet, anyway...

SILENCE FOR A MOMENT. KIP KEEPS LOOKING INTO THE DISTANCE AS BILL LOOKS OVER AT HIM. STUDYING HIM.

KIP   You don't know me. Haven't seen me before or anything...it's not that.

BILL   I didn't think so.

KIP   Doesn't matter how long you look at me or search your memory...you've never met me before this. (BEAT) Never once. (BEAT) I only live, like, six blocks away...but...

BILL   Look, what's this about? Honestly?

KIP   It's about you.

BILL   Me?

KIP   Yeah. About you...and my son. That's what I'm here about.

BILL LOOKS OVER AT KIP AND BLANCHES AT THIS. IN SILENCE.
BILL CAN'T HELP BUT SNEAK A LOOK AT HIS WATCH AGAIN.

BILL   ...I'm sorry, but my lunch is almost over and I need to go...this is, ummmmmmmmmm...I've got to...

KIP   You should probably take a long lunch.

BILL   What?

KIP   That's advice. Not a threat.

BILL   Yes, but...why would I...?

KIP   Because. You just should.

BILL   ...look...

KIP   Because I have some things to say to you and you need to hear them or I'm going to tell them to somebody else. Other people. People that you would probably not at all like me talking to...

BILL   ...

KIP   Does that make sense? (BEAT) Bill?

BILL DOESN'T RESPOND BUT SITS BACK ON HIS PARK BENCH AND WAITS. KIP LETS HIM STEW FOR A MOMENT. SILENCE.

BILL   Yes. I mean…yes. I suppose.

KIP   Yeah. It does. You know it does.

BILL   And who's your son? (BEAT) If I may ask?

KIP   Sure. You can ask…you just did. (BEAT) Or maybe you can guess. (BEAT) 'Taylor.' Taylor is my son. 'Taylor Simms.'

BILL   Oh.

KIP   Yeah. You know 'Taylor,' right? Adorable little guy…four years old. Blonde. You know which one. (BEAT) Right, Bill?

BILL   Yes…I mean…there's a boy who comes by here…with his mother…named 'Taylor.' Some afternoons. (BEAT) If that's who…

KIP   That's him.

BILL   …

KIP   He talks about you. Taylor does. (BEAT) Isn't that funny? He talks about you at home. When I get back from work. In the evening. After dinner. Sometimes during but mostly after…when I've got time to sit around and play with him at night…he talks about you.

BILL   …

KIP   My son talks about the 'nice man at the park.' (BEAT) Which is you, Bill. He is talking about you. (BEAT) Is he right? Do you think?

BILL   I'm sorry?

KIP   Is-he-right?

BILL   I don't know what you're asking me…

KIP   Are you a nice man? 'Bill Jensen?' (BEAT) Had to ask my wife your last name…she couldn't remember it at first…but hey.

BILL ...this is really outrageous, do you know that? (BEAT) It is. (BEAT) I mean it.

KIP Of course you do.

BILL I do! I mean...coming here, and, and...

KIP What?

BILL Just...talking to me like this!

KIP I haven't really said that much to you.

BILL Ha!

KIP Well, you can laugh and be whatever it is that you're acting like you are, but it's true. I've only said a couple things. And asked you a question... (BEAT) A question that you didn't answer yet.

BILL What?

KIP Are you 'nice?' Is my son right about you or not?

BILL Yes. (BEAT) I'm nice.

KIP Okay.

BILL I am.

KIP Fine.

BILL I'm a good person...

KIP Let's not get carried away there, Bill. All I asked was the 'nice' part. 'Good' is a whole different thing...

BILL Alright, well, I need to... (GATHERS UP HIS PAPER) ...you have a lovely family. Trish and your son. (BEAT) I mean that. (BEAT) I do.

KIP Uh-huh.

KIP AGREES WITH THIS. LOOKS OVER. MEETS BILL'S EYES.

BILL She's very sweet to talk with. Your wife.

KIP That's good.

BILL And your son...he's...

KIP I'm gonna stop you right there, Bill. You can stop talking. Right now.

BILL ...

KIP Because, see, I don't really give a shit if you like them or not. Honestly. Could not care less. (BEAT) The thing I do care about, though, is that you stop. That you just go away now...stop doing what you're doing with them. From this moment on. Got it? (BEAT) Do you get what I'm saying to you here, Bill? (BEAT) ...I want you to disappear.

BILL GLANCES OVER, TRYING TO QUICKLY ASSESS THIS MAN.

BILL Listen, I'm not...

KIP BILL.

BILL What?

KIP Do you get it? What I'm saying? I need an answer from you. Right here and now.

BILL Yes, but...listen...

KIP That's all that matters.

BILL No, I'm trying to say something now, so listen to me...please...

KIP Bill...just stop...

BILL No, I'm going to say something here! You are not going to railroad me with all of your tones and your...your accusations. (BEAT) I have done nothing wrong here...at all. Nothing. (BEAT) I have talked to your wife...to Trish...that is true, and your son as well...but there has been no wrong-doing of any kind. Of any kind. I didn't seek them out, I haven't...Trish speaks to me, if anything, she speaks to me and I'll tell you something, she is a lonely person. Maybe you don't like hearing that but it's true. She's lonely and she has sought out my friendship, not the other way around. Maybe you should speak to her about that at some point. Alright? About why she comes by in the afternoons.

KIP I see.

BILL And whatever you're implying about your son--about Taylor--is sickening to me...that is just...well, you really need to look at your own personal relation-ships, Mr. Simms. (BEAT) I'm sorry to be blunt like this, I'm not a rude person, but I can't listen to any more of this without defending myself. (STANDS) I think this is awful, what you've done, but I need to ask you to please tell your wife to leave me alone from now on. Alright? To go elsewhere in the park with your son, and I think that's unfortunate but that's the way it goes. Nothing to be done. (HE WAITS) And now I really do need to be...I've got to...

BILL STARTS TO WALK AWAY. KIP LETS HIM GET PRETTY FAR AND THEN CALLS OUT TO HIM:

KIP Oregon.

BILL STOPS IN HIS TRACKS. BACK TURNED TO KIP. STANDS IN SILENCE.

KIP I wasn't sure about it--I mean the photo...does kinda look like a younger you--but if just the word makes you stop like that...*Oregon*...then it must be you. (BEAT) Right?

BILL TURNS AND LOOKS AT KIP. KIP SITS THERE, WATCHING HIM AND WAITING BEFORE HE SAYS ANYTHING ELSE.

BILL No.

KIP No?

BILL That isn't me.

KIP Really?

BILL No, it's not.

KIP Huh. (BEAT) You know what? I think you're fulla shit, Bill...

BILL STANDS THERE, BLINKING AT HIM BUT SAYING NOTHING. HE LOOKS AROUND AND THINKS ABOUT LEAVING BUT DOESN'T.

KIP And anybody who wasn't full of shit--up to the fucking brim and overflow-ing--they would've walked away just now. Told me to 'go fuck myself' or spit in my face and marched right outta here. That's what they would've done...which leads me to believe that you are, in fact, THE 'Bill Jensen.' From the state of Oregon. From Eugene, Oregon. (BEAT) Aren't you, Bill?

BILL LOOKS SICK BUT CAN'T SAY A WORD. HE FINALLY NODS HIS HEAD WEAKLY.

KIP I don't know why they don't help you guys change your names when you move from spot to spot. State to state.

BILL ...

KIP I suppose that would defeat the purpose, though. Make it harder to track you from place to place. And that's the point. You need someone to keep an eye on you. Don't you? (BEAT) Bill?

BILL ...

KIP Because if not...if people just forgive and forget you...then you're free to do whatever it is you wanna do. Move from Oregon to here--well, with a few stops in-between, I imagine--get a job anywhere you like, go to the park on your lunchtime. (BEAT) If folks don't keep track of you then you can pretty much just go around acting like you're a normal guy. A nice guy. (BEAT) Isn't that right, 'Bill?' 'Bill Jensen' from Eugene, Oregon?

BILL But...that isn't me.

KIP No?

BILL No, it isn't. It's really not.

KIP You're not 'Bill Jensen' from Eugene? A guy whom I was able to track down from about fifty bucks worth of police records there on the internet? (BEAT) Hmmmmmmmmmm?

BILL No.

KIP It's pretty easy to prove, Bill.

BILL I'm saying I'm not that person any more.

KIP   Oh, I see. I see. So you're--it's more of a...philosophical response than the truth, is that what it is? Because you are the right guy. From that place. Who did what you did. In the past. (BEAT) A few times, even. (BEAT) You are.

BILL   But...that's not who I am now. Not now.

KIP   Ok, well, that's something we could talk about for a long time, I'm sure-- debate that issue for the rest of the year and we might not end up agreeing about that little fact--but you're the guy. From that website. That's what I'm saying. You're that man and I'm not sure that my wife or my son or your job would really be able to identify the subtleties that you're referring to. In your character. (BEAT) This 'new' you.

BILL LOOKS AT KIP. A DEEP SADNESS SETTLES OVER HIS FACE. TEARS IN HIS EYES, EVEN. KIP IS UNMOVED.

KIP   Do you get where I'm coming from here? Bill?

BILL   I'm a different person today.

KIP   Same name, though. If the authorities really felt the same way that you do...you think they'd make it like, umm, you know...the 'Witness Protection Program' or something...really help you disappear into a new identity or whatever. But they don't. Do they? (BEAT) No. They don't...

BILL   ...

KIP   ...and I think the reason that is, it's because you haven't really turned over a new leaf...gone through some big change and come out the other side a completely new and reformed person...I think you've been allowed to move out of their state, that's all. You've been plugged into the system and sent on your merry way to do as you please in some other state. With some other person's kids. Some unsuspecting grandparent or wife or whomever. That is what I think the situation is we find ourselves in here...'Bill.' From Oregon.

BILL   You don't know me, Mr. Simms. What I have gone through. What I live with. You don't and you never will... (BEAT) Not ever.

KIP   You're right. I don't because I'm not you or a person like you.

BILL STARTS TO SAY SOMETHING BUT KIP HOLDS UP A HAND AND STOPS HIM. KIP CONTINUES:

KIP That's the difference between me and you. No matter how much I work or how 'lonely' my wife is or the time I have to give up with my son because I'm out of town on a job somewhere...whatever shortcomings I have as a person and a man and a dad and a husband...I'm still nothing like you. (BEAT) Am I? (BEAT) Bill Jensen?

BILL No.

KIP Correct answer.

BILL You'll never be like me...and you don't know how lucky you are because of that. (BEAT) You'll never feel...what I carry around inside me. (BEAT) A sickness...

BILL LOOKS AT KIP AND TRIES TO HOLD HIS GAZE BUT HE CAN'T AND TURNS AWAY. PUTS HIS HEAD DOWN.

KIP I'm sure you're better. Right now. Sure that you're showing remarkable restraint these days. That's probably true. (BEAT) But so am I. I am restraining myself from moving over there next to you and pulling your cock out through your throat. That's what I wanna do. To you. But I'm not. No. Because I'm showing remarkable restraint.

KIP LETS THIS STAND FOR A MOMENT. FINALLY BILL SAYS:

BILL Look, Mr. Simms...I just wanna...please. (BEAT) I'm not saying any of this as an excuse or some kind of...as a sort of...reason for this, any of this...I sit on this bench most days, a lot of the time since I moved here, to this city, as a way to get away from people, not for a vantage point for...for...you know...I honestly don't. That's not what I do. I'm trying to be alone, to live a life where I'm alone and doing good...I said "I'm a good person" to you and I meant that. On the inside. Inside of me I am and I'm striving to be that. Now. Every day. (BEAT) I didn't ask your wife to be here when I was here. I didn't want your son to run up the hill one day and sit there...on my bench...and to smile over at me and laugh and, and...I didn't do anything to make that happen. It's not fair. It's not fair to me. (BEAT) What I've done is in the past and it's not fair to punish me like this. What you are saying to me...doing to me here. (BEAT) Please. I'm not asking you to understand me or who I am or what I've done...but can't you see that it's not right...to...for you to do this to me? (BEAT) Can't you?

KIP No.

KIP SHAKES HIS HEAD AND LOOKS RIGHT INTO BILL'S EYES.

BILL 'No?'

KIP I hear you, what you've just said...but I can't feel that. Inside me. That what I'm telling you is wrong. (BEAT) What's wrong is that I'm not gonna tell some-body what you're doing with your afternoons--that's wrong. I'm remiss in not letting anyone at your place of work know about who you are and what secrets are hidden away in your past. (BEAT) I'm letting you go...like the police and the social workers who I condemned before. I'm telling you to go away, to run off and bother some other family or co-worker or innocent child. That's what I'm doing. That is what I'll get to live with and probably pick up the paper one day and see your face there, in a photo, blinking back at me...like you are right now... with that 'what have I done?' look on your fucking face...*that* is the mistake I'm about to make. (BEAT) But I can live with that.

BILL ...please...Kip...

KIP Bill. Don't. (BEAT) Trish has no idea that I'm doing this. Obviously neither does Taylor. I don't want their lives changed one iota from what it was since the last day they came here. (BEAT) But you will go away. Elsewhere. You will.

BILL ...

KIP You hear me? (BEAT) Huh? (BEAT) BILL?

BILL And...I mean...if I don't? What then?

KIP I'll kill you. I'm not joking and I'm not a violent person...I didn't grow up in a house like that but I'm gonna come back here...this week and a month from now...three years...doesn't matter. I will be back. Occasionally and often. And if I find you here, sitting in the sunlight and reading your paper and listening to the children playing...I-will-kill-you. You understand me? Kill you dead.

BILL Yes.

KIP STRETCHES AND BILL FLINCHES AT THIS. KIP DOESN'T DO IT TO INTIMI-DATE BILL BUT HE DOESN'T HATE THE RESULT.

KIP So you decide. Bill. What you want to do next. Think about that while you're here and the sun is warming your face…think about if it's worth it or not…for you to ever come back here again. (BEAT) Ok?

BILL I've done nothing wrong.

KIP Alright.

BILL I have done nothing to your family that is wrong…I've…I've…I've…

KIP Fine.

BILL I haven't!

KIP Whatever you say, Bill.

BILL Your wife talks to me!

KIP Uh-huh.

BILL She keeps coming here to speak with me about things. Not the other way around.

KIP I hear you.

BILL Your son ran up the hill…from there…right over there, the first time. Ran up here to me! Where I was already sitting!

KIP Right.

BILL He came running to me. Up here to me and sat on my bench. (POINTING) Right there.

BILL IS TRYING TO GET THROUGH TO KIP BUT IT DOESN'T SEEM TO BE WORKING. SUDDENLY, KIP TURNS AND GRABS BILL BY BOTH LAPELS. PULLS HIM CLOSE. FACE TO FACE. SHAKES HIM ONCE. TWICE. HARD. SILENCE AS KIP LETS THIS MOMENT OF RESTRAINED VIOLENCE SPEAK FOR ITSELF. THEN:

KIP   I understand. (BEAT) And you understand me, too, right? Don't you, Bill? (BEAT) You do...don't you? (BEAT) DON'T YOU?

BILL   ...yes.

KIP   Then good.

KIP NODS AND LETS BILL GO. KIP REACHES OVER, PATS BILL ON THE LEG, AND THEN GETS UP.

KIP   ...beautiful day, huh? (BEAT) Gorgeous.

KIP MOVES AWAY AND EXITS. BILL SITS THERE, WITH A HANDFUL OF TOYS AND HIS NEWSPAPER. SUDDENLY HIS FACE REDDENS. TWISTED. ANGRY. ASHAMED. HURT. HE HAS BEEN CAUGHT OUT AND HE IS FURIOUS. HE BURSTS INTO TEARS. SOBS FOR A MOMENT. ALONE ON THE BENCH.

BILL   (to himself) ...I've done nothing wrong...I've done nothing wrong here...I've done nothing wrong...I've done nothing...nothing...

BILL STOMPS HIS FEET AND WRAPS HIS ARMS AROUND HIS CHEST. TRYING TO COMFORT HIMSELF. HOLDING BACK A SCREAM. TEARS RUNNING DOWN HIS CHEEKS. THE NEWSPAPER AND TOYS SPILL OUT OF HIS HANDS AND ONTO THE GROUND AT HIS FEET.

BILL   (to himself) ...nothing....nothing...nothing...!! (BEAT) I HAVE DONE NOTH-ING WRONG!!!!

HE SITS THERE, FIGHTING TO REGAIN HIS COMPOSURE. HOLDING HIMSELF. ROCKING BACK AND FORTH. THE SOUND OF CHILDREN PLAYING IN THE DIS-TANCE. GROWING.

KANDAHAR

KANDAHAR had its world premiere at the Gaslight Theater as part of the 'LaBute New Theater Festival' in St. Louis Missouri in July 2015 and subsequently at the 59E59 street theaters in New York as part of the 'NYC LaBute New Theater Festival' in January 2016. Both were directed by John Pierson.

Man – Michael Hogan

Michael Hogan
Photo: STLAS

A MAN SITTING IN A CHAIR. STARING STRAIGHT AHEAD. A HARSH LIGHT IN HIS FACE. HE DOESN'T SEEM TO MIND. HE SITS IN SILENCE FOR A MOMENT OR TWO. DRUMMING FINGERS ON THE TABLE TO A BEAT IN HIS HEAD. FINALLY:

MAN   ...she made me do it. (BEAT) And I know you hear people say that, all the time, but it's true. She *made* me. Somehow she did. I know she did. She made all of it happen. All this. (BEAT) Women have that power...you know what I mean? They do...it's, like, a secret power inside of 'em. They really do have it, I'm not just saying that or, you know...using it as an excuse...I've always felt that and it's true. They have this thing inside them, this way of being and thinking and acting...and they use it on us to get us to do stuff without us guys even realizing it. It's true. That's a real phenomenon. Their mysterious ways. My dad, he told me about it and I believe he was accurate...to some degree, at least. (BEAT) Anyway, if that's true or it's not--in a general sense, I mean--I still believe that she made me do all the stuff that's happened here. I'm saying in a more specific way. What I've done...how I went off and, you know...all the damage I did...that was her doing...she brought that down upon herself. And me. And everybody else.

HE WAITS. THINKING. WATCHING. MOTIONLESS IN HIS CHAIR.

She planted those seeds in my head--what set me off, made me go ballistic, is what I'm saying--long before I ever went over for my last tour. Over there to Kandahar. (BEAT) Even before I left I was thinking those things. Thinking about doing that stuff. To her. To her and some people. Other people that we knew in our lives. I swear I was. (BEAT) She has a way of getting inside my head...getting in there and forcing me to do things for her...and to her...things that I never could've even dreamed about when I was a kid. No way. Uh-uh. Some of that shit was stuff I never could've come up with on my own...or as a child. No. It took a woman like her to make me have any of those type thoughts. (BEAT) Seriously.

HE WIPES AT HIS EYES. BLINKING. TRYING TO CONCENTRATE ON WHAT HE'S SAYING.

And I was a good kid, too. Everybody said that...when I was younger? Everybody did. I was, like, a nice boy. Not a gold star type child, not like that, or some fancy straight A student--in fact, my dad even had one of those things, those stickers for your car, a bumper sticker, that he found at a truck stop somewhere, and it said--this was on an old Monte Carlo he would drive around--he had this sticker and it read: "MY KID BEATS UP HONOR ROLL STUDENTS AT JEFFERSON JUNIOR HIGH." That made him laugh, that fucking sticker did. He would see that, no matter when, and he would bust out laughing and he had a big laugh, this guy. My dad. This loud sorta laugh that came outta him and could take over a room or on the street or wherever. He loved that thing. But it wasn't true; about me hurting other kids or that type of deal. I was nice back then. A really nice guy in those days...in high school, too. For that matter. Really good to all the others around me--and I was in class with some real dicks, too, so...but yeah, I was very respectful and all that shit. I mean, pretty much. Everybody has their days but overall, that's what I'm saying is overall...I was a good person. That's from my mom, that side of me...I should be clear about that, she was the person who brought out the sunnier side of me at that age, not my dad. He didn't do shit for me. Ever. Except laugh at that fucking bumper sticker of his... (BEAT) But see? I'm not blaming all women for what's happened to me, or saying that they're all crazy or psycho or whatnot, I'm not. I like women. My mom was a real great lady and I loved her. Right up to the moment she passed...and I mean there on her hospital bed...I was blown away by her. As a person. Yeah. She was great. (BEAT) Women are just fine...but they do have those powers I was talking about earlier. They really do.

HE NODS AT THIS, DRIFTING OFF AS HE THINKS ABOUT HER OR SOMETHING ELSE. SILENT FOR A BEAT.

But that's not why I'm here...right? Why you got me sitting here and talking. You want some answers to what happened, don't you? Over there at the base yesterday...that's what we're doing here, am I right? Sure. I get it. I understand. And that's cool by me. It is. (BEAT) I already told you about my wife...what she was able to do to me...how she can make me feel with just one word, or, like, not even that...without a single word spoken. No. Just a look. She can look at me and make me so fucking hot for her or, you know, angry or happy...that's what she can do. Since the day I met her. Yeah. (BEAT) And she likes it...enjoys it...that power over me. She does. Turns it off and on like some light switch or not even that, the kind that doesn't even need a switch...you just clap your hands and the lights go off and on. (CLAPS HIS HANDS) BAM!! (CLAPS AGAIN) Like that. (CLAPS AGAIN) BAM!! Off and on. Off and on. That's what she'd do to me...just by looking me in the eye. Just like that product you've seen on TV... (CLAPS HIS HANDS) BAM! BAM! BAM!

HE STOPS AND FIDGETS FOR A MOMENT. TAKE A SIP OF WATER FROM A GLASS IN FRONT OF HIM. SMILES.

You probably don't believe that. Don't wanna believe that she could do a thing like that to me...or care that she's got that ability. That doesn't answer all of your questions...doesn't close the book on your investigations...right? No. That doesn't do the trick, I'm sure. You need the HOWS and WHYS and all that shit from me before we're through and that's okay. I get it. I knew we'd end up over here, somehow I already knew that...that we'd have to do this part at some point. Based on what I did. And all that. (BEAT) Lemme ask you something...you've seen combat, right, all of you? (WAITS) Yeah? (WAITS) Okay then. (BEAT) You ever kill anybody? Any of you? (BEAT) I guess you wouldn't tell me if you had... or don't want to, maybe, but I bet at least a few of you have...probably more. Overseas or over there on the base. Some guy like me, did shit to people...no doubt you've had to bring him down. Take 'em out. No doubt about it. Of course you have. Come on...you can tell me. (BEAT) I'm just asking...

HE WAITS ANOTHER BEAT. NOTHING IN RETURN. HE SHRUGS AS HE SITS QUIETLY.

Whatever. Doesn't matter. Can't change at all what I've done, but I just thought we might talk about it, compare stories and that sorta thing, but it's no big deal...doesn't alter the facts. Right? Nope. Not one little bit. (BEAT) There was this guy I got deployed with, that last time. And she started in with him. Messing around. You know what I'm saying...right? You've checked all that out already. That side of the story. About him. And her. What they've done. Sure you have. (BEAT) I'm not saying she picked him, like, chose him over some of the other guys because she knew we'd end up together over there but you have to won- der...don't you? You have to know that's gonna run in and out of your brain a thousand times, whether she's really that cold or not. Capable of such calibrated shit or not...wait, that's not the right word...not that...I mean 'calculated.' Don't I?

Yeah, I think so. If she could be that mean...and calculated...and all that... (BEAT) And yes is the answer, if you're asking. She could do that and then some. That's just her nature. To be that way. To hurt me. (BEAT) But I got her back, though... didn't I? Got her back and then some... (BEAT) Yep. I sure did.

HE SMILES A LITTLE, TO HIMSELF. AS IF HE'S SAVORING A PRIVATE JOKE. AND THEN IT PASSES. HE BEGINS IN AGAIN:

Over there in Afghanistan, it's like...you know...the Wild West or some shit. I mean that. Not that they don't have a lotta, like, restaurants and, you know, snack foods and places for Wi-Fi and all that stuff, because they do. They totally do, but it's just...different. Walking on a street and you never know what's gonna happen next. A car blows up, some kid is gonna try to give you broken glass in a soda pop...it's just day-by-day when you serve in a place like that. Not sure who cares or wants to kill you. That's just how it is. (BEAT) And a guy can get himself shot over there, real easy. Or whatever. Captain was always saying that to us, and this doctor that I was seeing...not just me but a lot of guys, 'cause of the stress and, you know...just because. They were always telling us to be alert but to try and relax. Yeah, that's a good idea! I mean, what the fuck? How are you gonna do those two things at once? Huh? I dunno. Doesn't matter. (BEAT) I found an email from her--my wife--to this guy one time, he got up from one of the base computers there, stood up from his seat and walked away...I wandered over to use it next, I swear I wasn't following him or trying to see what he was up to, but the guy forgot to log out and so all his shit is...you know...it's right there... so I flicked through his things and there it was. From her. HOTLIPS69. (BEAT) The first part came from that one show about the hospital. M*A*S*H. That's where she got that. The '69' is probably sort of self-explanatory...she thought it was funny. (BEAT) I read the thing a couple times. Print it off. Carry it around in my wallet. (LOOKING OUT) You've got my stuff, right? It's in there if you wanna read it. (BEAT) Doesn't say too much. Weather back home. A couple bits about working at the Commissary, which she did for awhile, and then a few lines about him. And her. And his cock. And a little part about his upcoming birthday. (BEAT) Anyway, the whole thing's just so fucking pathetic...right? So usual and normal. Shit happens all the time, and people go on with their lives...and so the captain keeps telling me to take it easy and the doctor is always asking questions as he gives me another bottle to fill up with my piss...after a month or two, it starts to wear you down. (BEAT) I probably shot about seven or eight guys while I was in Kandahar...maybe ten...and almost every one of 'em was in an actual firefight... but I gotta admit, since we're here now and this is the time for it, I guess...I was practicing on a couple of 'em. I was. I'm not ashamed to say that, or...angry or sad, even...I guess I don't feel very much about it at all. It's just the truth so I thought I should let you know...that's what happened and that's what I did. (BEAT) I did that. I practiced...

HE STARES OUT AT THE LIGHT. SQUINTING. TAKES A DRINK AND THEN CONTINUES.

When we got back to the States--me and my company, I'm saying--I spent a nice couple days with my wife. She was sweet and seemed happy to see me. In her way. But I knew what was up...how she really felt...about me. And us. And all that. (BEAT) I fucked her that first night I was home but it was dark in the room so I couldn't really see her face and she couldn't see mine--I think she liked it, but who knows? How can you ever really tell with somebody? Ask 'em, I guess... or listen to 'em, during it, I mean...but who knows what's really in their hearts? (BEAT) Not me. Don't ask me...

THE MAN STRETCHES A BIT. STOPS. LOOKING AROUND. FINALLY HE STARTS IN AGAIN.

Anyway, yeah...one morning I got up and made breakfast--I've always been a pretty early riser--and I ate and cleaned it up and all that, and then I took that email outta my wallet and put it there on her pillow, next to her. So she'd see it as she woke up. (BEAT) She slept late, the way she always did...but I was there on the bed. Waiting. When she finally did...eyes fluttering open really slowly, the first thing she saw was that paper. The words she'd written, right there next to her face. Her eyes focused on it--I had promised myself to wait until she did-- and she was right here... (INDICATING) ...turned away from me a little bit...but I could feel her pupils getting a little bigger as she's recognizing the thing in front of her...and she turns over, turns right to where I'm kneeling on the comforter... and I smiled at her. Without a word. Just that one smile...as I put my bayonet in her throat. Put it in there a couple times. Real fast, like this. (INDICATES)

So she couldn't speak. (BEAT) I watched her dying, on our bed there, as her mouth opened up a couple times, trying to say a word or two...something...but she never got that far. There was just this whistling sound coming out. Through the holes I'd made. In her neck. (BEAT) And after that I loaded up and headed over to the Mess Hall and did what I did. To whoever was there. (WAITS) He was, wasn't he? With a bunch of those assholes from 'D' Company...I made sure I got to them first and the rest...well...that just happened. And I'm sorry about that. (BEAT) Like I said before...they teach you this shit and then they expect you can just switch it on and off. (CLAPS HIS HANDS) BAM!!! Just like that. But you can't. It's not that easy...women can, maybe. Because of their powers. But not us...not guys...or at least not me.

HE STOPS FOR A MOMENT. COLLECTS HIMSELF. LOOKING STRAIGHT AHEAD.

I don't have any special powers. Or stuff like that. I don't. I hear voices once in a while, or maybe it's just the wind. I'm not sure. Doesn't matter. (BEAT) You guys will do what you've gotta do...just like I did. That's the point and I'm sure you understand it, whether you wanna tell me you do or not. You know it's true. I had to do what I did. She did what she had to do and that motherfucker from my outfit, he did what he had to do, too. That's the way life works. You do what you gotta do. You do it because you want to or need to or for no damn reason at all. Sometimes you get away with it and life goes on...but sometimes you don't. You get hit by a car or used for target practice while you're walking down some dusty street in a place called 'Kandahar.' We live in a random fucking time and we just keep on spinning the wheel and throwing the dice and we shouldn't be surprised when our turn is up. But we are. We always are. (BEAT) I could see it in her eyes...she was very surprised. So were the guys over there...across the street...when I walked inside and they were laughing and eating their goddamn *omelets*...they were very fucking surprised, too...for about two seconds...and then they were dead and it didn't really matter whether they were surprised or not. (BEAT) And when the time comes for me...when you do what you have to do, what I know you'll do...I guess I might be surprised as well. That it's my turn now...that it's finally here...but I really shouldn't be. Should I? (BEAT) No. I really shouldn't be at all...

HE LOOKS OUT INTO THE LIGHT AGAIN. SMILES. NODS AT THIS.

Well, who knows? Maybe I will be or maybe I won't. (BEAT) I guess we'll just have to wait and see...won't we?

THE MAN PUTS HIS HEAD DOWN NOW. AWAY FROM THE LIGHT. HE BEGINS TO DRUM HIS FINGERS ON THE TABLE. TO A BEAT THAT ONLY HE CAN HEAR. IN HIS HEAD.

LIFE MODEL

LIFE MODEL had its world premiere at the Gaslight Theater as part of the 'LaBute New Theater Festival' in St. Louis Missouri in July 2016. It was directed by John Pierson.

Artist: Jenny Smith
Model: Bridget Bassa

(left to right) Jenny Smith, Bridget Bassa
Photo: Patrick Huber

NICE APARTMENT IN A CITY SOMEWHERE. LIGHT STREAMS IN THROUGH LARGE WINDOWS ON ONE WALL. A HALLWAY LEADS TO SEVERAL OTHER ROOMS. BIG PLACE. AN ARTIST (40S) SITTING IN A STRAIGHT-BACK CHAIR. DRAWING PAD IN ONE HAND AND RESTING ON A KNEE. SHE FAVORS CHAR-COALS AND IS EVEN NOW HARD AT WORK. MUSIC PLAYING. SOMETHING NICE. A MODEL (20S) SEATED IN FRONT OF HER. NAKED. A FEW TATTOOS. SHE'S IN A POSE AND HOLDING IT. LOOKING AT THE AUDIENCE. THIS GOES ON FOR QUITE SOME TIME. A FEW MINUTES AT LEAST. AFTER A MOMENT, THE TING! OF AN EGG TIMER. THE MODEL STOPS AND STRETCHES. THE ARTIST DOES THE SAME. THEY SMILE AT EACH OTHER AND BOTH STAND UP. THE MODEL SLIPS ON A ROBE AND THE ARTIST TAKES A DRINK.

ARTIST   ...that's lovely.

MODEL   Thank you.

ARTIST   I'm serious, though. Really really nice today. Some great moments.

MODEL   Thank you.

ARTIST   Hard as hell to capture, but great!

MODEL   Ha! Yeah...that's...art is amazing.

ARTIST   Yes, it really is. It's amazing.

MODEL   Yep.

ARTIST   Are you...I mean, outside of here, are you interested in it? At all?

MODEL   You know...like...yeah. Some.

ARTIST   Really?

MODEL   Not to do or anything...not what you do, obviously...but yeah, I used to draw when I was younger, took art in school--high school--and I know a few artists or I've gone through books of their pictures and stuff...museums.

ARTIST   Oh, so you're...that's great.

MODEL   Yeah. Exhibitions that I'm aware of from the subway, or...you know, posters on the side of buses that catch my eye or something. (BEAT) I saw a Peter Max thingie recently...at MOMA. Is that his name? Marx or Max? (BEAT)

Max, I think...

ARTIST   Yes, Peter Max! I saw that, too! I mean, went for the Lichtenstein, obviously...but I did pop in and check out the Max as well. (SMILES) So fun. So kitschy.

MODEL   Uh-huh. You're right. It's fun...lots of color.

ARTIST   Yes. He was big on that. Color.

MODEL   Yep. (BEAT) It reminded me of that...you know, that one movie...

ARTIST   Which?

MODEL   The one that The Beatles did. The cartoon one.

ARTIST   Oh, right, yes! YELLOW SUBMARINE.

MODEL   That's it, yeah...doesn't it seem like that? A little bit?

ARTIST   Absolutely...I think he even had something to do with it...or...now I'm not sure, but I know he knew The Beatles. John, at least. (BEAT) John was an artist, too. Did you know that? Not amazing, but still...he dabbled in it...

MODEL   Huh.

ARTIST   He even had a psychedelic car...John did...and I think Peter Max might've done the design for that as well...I can't remember now... (BEAT) I might be mixing that up.

MODEL   Doesn't matter.

ARTIST   No, but...it's interesting. (BEAT) So you do like art?

MODEL   Yep. It's great...

ARTIST   I agree. It can be. Hard work at times...obviously...but...great.

MODEL   Yeah, no, that's true. When I see you going at it, concentrating like that--I can tell that you're really trying to get it right.

ARTIST   Well, that's all part of it...

MODEL   True. (BEAT) It's cool.

ARTIST   Thanks...

THEY NOD AT EACH OTHER AND SHE POINTS TOWARD THE HALLWAY AS SHE STARTS TO MOVE OFF. TOUCHES THE MODEL ON THE SHOULDER.

ARTIST   Anyway! If you'd like a drink...

MODEL   No, that's okay...

ARTIST   You should have something...it's a lot of energy up there...doing...

MODEL   ...nothing...?

ARTIST   Ha! No, it's not nothing! I know that for sure...it's hard work...

MODEL   It is, actually.

ARTIST   I know it. I could never do it...

MODEL   Oh no, you probably could...

ARTIST   No, not posing...I mean 'exposing' myself...that part of it. Being so free with my body like that...

MODEL   Oh, I see. Yeah, there is that part of it... (BEAT) Anyway, it's a lot harder than I thought it'd be when I first read the ad. The posing.

ARTIST   Is that right?

MODEL   I mean, I had some friends do it in college...for a class or, you know, to make a little money...

ARTIST   ...right...

MODEL   But this is...sometimes you really have to concentrate to hold a pose for that long...or you start to get all... (SHE MIMES FEELING CONFINED) You know what I mean?

ARTIST   Absolutely! I absolutely do--that's why we take the breaks. Scheduled and on time. Because I sympathize.

MODEL   Yeah. I appreciate that...

ARTIST   Of course. Now, if you'll excuse me for a moment, I'm going to use the little girl's room. (POINTS) Relax.

MODEL   Thanks...

SHE PLOPS DOWN ON A COUCH AND STRETCHES. THE ARTIST POINTS TO THE KITCHEN AGAIN. ANOTHER QUICK TOUCH BETWEEN THEM. CASUAL.

ARTIST   And do have something to drink! It really does help...I have some wine and there's grape juice...water...even a 7-up, I think. Might be one of those diet kind, though...take a look and grab whatever!

SHE SMILES AND EXITS. THE MODEL STRETCHES AGAIN AND FINALLY GETS UP, GOES TO THE KITCHEN. RUMMAGES AROUND. COMES BACK WITH THE 7-UP. SHE SITS AGAIN BUT NEARER THE ARTIST'S CHAIR THIS TIME. SHE REACHES OVER AND FLIPS OPEN HER SKETCH PAD. GLANCES AT THE WORK. INTEREST-ED, SHE PICKS IT UP AND FLIPS THROUGH THE PICTURES INSIDE. SLOWLY AT FIRST, THEN PICKING UP SPEED. THE MODEL TOSSES IT BACK ON THE CHAIR AND GETS TO HER FEET. SHE LOOKS AROUND AND CROSSES TO A SET OF SHELVES. LOTS OF BOOKS BUT DOZENS OF SIMILAR ART PADS TUCKED INTO ONE SPACE AS WELL. SHE PULLS ONE OUT. HURRIES THROUGH IT. ANOTHER ONE. THEN ONE MORE. SHE REPLACES THEM AND THEN LOOKS AROUND THE ROOM. TAKING IN DEEP BREATHS. SHE GOES TO A PILE OF CLOTHES ON ONE CHAIR. DROPS THE ROBE AND PULLS ON HER PANTS AND A T-SHIRT. SHE IS GETTING INTO HER SHOES WHEN THE ARTIST RETURNS. A MOMENT OF SILENCE.

THE ARTIST STOPS, SEEING THAT THE MODEL IS DRESSING. WAITS UNTIL SHE TURNS TO HER AS SHE CONTINUES TO PULL ON HER CHUCK TAYLOR BASKET-BALL SHOES. THE ARTIST TRIES TO DECIDE WHAT TO SAY FIRST BUT INSTEAD SHE POINTS AT THE MODEL'S DRINK.

ARTIST)   Cherry.

MODEL   (STARTLED) Sorry? What?

SHE POINTS AGAIN AT THE CAN THE MODEL HAS PLACED ON A TABLE.

ARTIST   Your drink.

MODEL   'Cherry?'

ARTIST   It was 'Cherry.' Not diet. It was a Cherry 7-Up.

MODEL   Right.

ARTIST   Not the other kind. (BEAT) Thought it was 'diet' but it's not…it's that. (BEAT) Cherry. (BEAT) As I get older I'm losing my memory for little things like that. Details.

MODEL   Yeah.

ARTIST   Is it good? The 'Cherry' one?

MODEL   Ummmmm…yeah…pretty okay…

ARTIST   Good. I'm glad. (SMILES) At least it's not diet!

THEY STAND LOOKING AT EACH OTHER FOR ANOTHER MOMENT, THEN SHE CONTINUES TO GET DRESSED.

MODEL   …I'm just gonna go. Okay?

ARTIST   Why? What's the…?

MODEL   Let's just leave it there.

ARTIST   But…

MODEL   You know what? You don't even owe me for today…I'll throw that in for free, but…I need to go.

ARTIST   I don't understand. What's the…?

MODEL   I just need to.

ARTIST   Okay.

MODEL   Thanks.

THE ARTIST KEEPS HER DISTANCE AND LETS THE MODEL KEEP GATHERING HER STUFF BUT SHE DOES SPEAK AGAIN:

ARTIST   Did I say something…or…?

MODEL   No…I just have to go.

ARTIST   Well...that's not true, but...

MODEL   (TURNING QUICKLY) It isn't?

ARTIST   I mean...you're the one who said we could do today, so I think it's... you know...odd that suddenly, after our little break time...that all of a sudden you have to leave. (BEAT) It's not impossible but it's kind of unlikely. (BEAT) Did you get a call or something? A text that was--

MODEL   No.

ARTIST   I didn't think so...

MODEL   It's not that. I just...

ARTIST   So that's why I'm asking you if I did something wrong or not? Said a word to you that wasn't... (HOLDING UP HER HANDS) I've always tried to be very respectful with you during our times together...is that true or not?

MODEL   You have, yeah.

ARTIST   Okay. Good. (BEAT) With you and my other model--the guy who comes on occasion--I feel like I'm very good to both of you in that way.

MODEL   I'd say that's true...for the most part, yes.

ARTIST   'The most part?'

MODEL   I mean...yes. Fine. You are. Outside of just the...you know...the weirdness of doing this, yes, you have been. (BEAT) It's not that.

ARTIST   I'm glad.

MODEL   I mean...

ARTIST   What?

MODEL   I just think...

ARTIST   Please. Tell me if I've...

MODEL   No, I should probably just...

ARTIST   Please.

SHE STOPS FOR A MOMENT AND TURNS TO THE ARTIST. IF SHE WANTS TO KNOW SO BAD THEN SHE'LL TELL HER. WHY NOT?

MODEL   I don't think you're being honest with me.

ARTIST   Sorry? What does that mean? How am I not being honest...?

MODEL   Show me your thing there...

ARTIST   (LOOKING AROUND) What?

MODEL   Your thing! The thingie!

ARTIST   I don't even know what that...?

MODEL   Your pad! The art pad thingie that you're drawing in...show it to me.

THE ARTIST STOPS AT THIS. LOOKS OVER AT HER MODEL VERY SLOWLY AND CAREFULLY. A LONG BEAT GOES BY.

ARTIST   No.

MODEL   Okay...

ARTIST   Not possible.

MODEL   Then I'm going...

ARTIST   I don't show my work.

MODEL   ...alright...

ARTIST   I've told you that. Many times.

MODEL   I know, but I need to see it now...

ARTIST   No, I won't do that.

MODEL   Fine. (TURNS TO GO) Goodbye...

ARTIST   It's not you. I mean to anybody. I don't display. I don't do shows or that kind of thing...not ever.

MODEL I'm not asking that. I'm saying let me take a glance inside your book.

ARTIST No, that's not right. It's not for you...or anyone...it's private.

MODEL Fine, then...I'll leave.

SHE NOW HAS HER STUFF. A COAT AND BAGS AND LOTS OF CRAP TO CARRY BUT SHE'S READY TO GO.

ARTIST I'm...this is so strange! I mean, I've never seen you like this before... all...

MODEL Yeah, well...

ARTIST I'm...I dunno, I feel sort of...do you want more, is that it? (BEAT) Or... is it something else?

MODEL More what...?

ARTIST Money! Obviously...is that why you got yourself dressed and are storming out of here...you want more of a payment or something? What is it? (BEAT) I pay better than my friends do...I promise you that...

MODEL ...no, it's not...

ARTIST Or the classes in town...over at the university...half as much as I pay. For *two* hour sessions.

MODEL ...

ARTIST Not by the hour. Not like this.

MODEL I understand. It's not that...

ARTIST It's not money?

MODEL It's not. No.

ARTIST And it's not me...? I mean, that's what you said...that I didn't...

MODEL No, it's not...I mean, yes, it's you, but you didn't do anything wrong... like sexual, or that sort of thing...I'm not saying that...

ARTIST Okay. (BEAT) Well...if you can't tell me and I don't know what it is, then

I guess we'll just have to...whatever. Leave it, I suppose.

MODEL   That's fine.

THE ARTIST GOES TO A COUNTER AND GRABS HER PURSE. STARTS TO COUNT OUT SOME BILLS.

MODEL   I said you didn't need to give...

ARTIST   I insist on paying you for the work you've done. (THINKING) That was an hour, so here's fifty...and here...another for what I'd already had you booked for next time...

MODEL   Don't be silly. Next time?

ARTIST   Just let me do what I want, please, and then we'll be square. (GIVING HER MONEY) There. Finished.

MODEL   I peeked.

ARTIST   Excuse me?

MODEL   I looked at your book...there. The pad. (BEAT) When you were peeing.

ARTIST   Oh.

MODEL   Yeah, so. (BEAT) Sorry.

ARTIST   That's...I see. (BEAT) I see.

MODEL   I know.

ARTIST   ...

MODEL   I never have before, but it was...just right there...and...so...

ARTIST   Like Bluebeard's Castle, huh?

MODEL   I'm...I don't know what that means.

ARTIST   Good. (BEAT) Probably for the best.

MODEL   ...okay...

THE MODEL SHRUGS AND THEN TRIES TO EXPLAIN HERSELF A BIT MORE:

MODEL)   Only a few pages. At first...and...then suddenly...I couldn't stop.

SHE WAITS AND LET'S THIS SINK IN. THE ARTIST ABSORBS IT ALL.

ARTIST   I only asked one thing of you and that was it...one little thing and you couldn't...even...

MODEL   I know.

ARTIST   To just...do the job and let me do mine and...I don't share my work.

MODEL   Yeah. (BEAT) I see why. Now.

ARTIST   And what's that supposed to mean?

MODEL   Nothing...just that...you're...

ARTIST   What?

MODEL   It's bad! I mean...it's...

ARTIST   It's abstract...

MODEL   No, it's just bad. Plain old 'bad.'

ARTIST   You can stop now...

MODEL   I was surprised, actually. Really surprised by it, to be honest...

ARTIST   Fine...let's drop it. Alright?

MODEL   The way you carry on...with all the set-up and everything...sizing it up as we're getting started...and how you study me...make such a big deal of it... laying out all your stuff. Your...little...chalks.

ARTIST   They're charcoals, actually. That's my medium. (BEAT) *Charcoal*.

MODEL   What is?

ARTIST   What I use. Those. (POINTS) Those are charcoals...and some pastels.

MODEL   I see. Ok. Fine. Your pastels. It's very childish...for a person your age, I mean. For an adult.

ARTIST *Thank you.*

MODEL Not what you use, I don't mean...but your work. It's just...bad.

ARTIST Great. So...you're, like, a critic, now, too...on top of a cheat? You think you can criticize my work...evaluate it like a professional?

MODEL No...it's just my opinion, but...you're even worse than *me*!

ARTIST Terrific. (BEAT) You should go.

MODEL Fine...but...

ARTIST I'm not really interested in your analysis...I mean...God...!

SHE LOOKS AT THE ARTIST A BIT LONGER, THEN GRABS HER PURSE AND GOES FOR THE DOOR. THE ARTIST STOPS HER WITH:

ARTIST And that's really why you're going? Because of how bad my work is...? You packed up because of that?

MODEL Yes.

ARTIST That's absurd.

MODEL No, it's not!

ARTIST I mean...why would that even matter to you...actually? I don't get it. Why would you care? It pays whether I'm any good at it or not...

MODEL I understand that.

ARTIST You sit on your ass and I pay you. Who gives a shit how the work is?

MODEL I do, I guess.

ARTIST Ha! What, you only wanna be drawn by a good artist...is that it?

MODEL No. (BEAT) By an *artist*. (BEAT) Someone who actually is one...

ARTIST I don't even know what that means!

MODEL You know what I'm saying...

ARTIST No, I don't...I really don't...

MODEL Yes, you do...come on!

ARTIST What?!

MODEL I'm saying that you're not really a person who does this...not even as a hobby. You're not.

ARTIST That's insane! We've been meeting for five months now...every Saturday for five months...and I have been sitting in that chair, right there, and spending that time with charcoal in my hand or a pastel and drawing your body so...I think that I'm pretty much an artist...whether you think so or not...!

MODEL No, you're not! You're not!

ARTIST This is just...nuts...

MODEL I looked over there, too...

THE ARTIST STOPS AT THIS SUGGESTION. FOLLOWS THE MODEL'S GAZE TO-WARD THE SHELF FULL OF ART PADS ACROSS THE ROOM.

ARTIST You did what?

MODEL I looked! Over there...at some of those pads in there, your finished ones...and I can tell--even *I* can tell--that you're not an artist. You're just not.

ARTIST I don't even know what to say...

MODEL The truth. (BEAT) Just say that.

ARTIST I'm...I've been doing this...self-taught, yes, but doing it...for a very long time...and I don't want to discuss my work with you...some no-one...I'm not going to do that!

MODEL Fine. Okay. If that's your story, then stick with it...that's fine.

ARTIST That isn't a story, it's the truth!

THE MODEL SUDDENLY MOVES TO THE COUCH AND PICKS UP THE PAD. OPENS IT AND HOLDS TWO PAGES OUT TO THE ARTIST. SQUIGGLES. LINES. A SMUDGE OR TWO THAT MIGHT HAVE PROMISE BUT FOR THE MOST PART, IT'S DECIDEDLY PRIMITIVE.

ARTIST   Put that down, please! Stop! Stop it!

MODEL   No, look at it...look! LOOK AT IT!

ARTIST   Put it down! That's my property and you have no right to...stop it! PUT IT DOWN! NOW!!!

THE ARTIST MOVES AT THE MODEL AND SHE BACKS AWAY. TURNING ANOTHER PAGE SO THE ARTIST CAN LOOK AT IT. MAKING HER SEE WHAT'S THERE. SOME CRUDE LINE DRAWINGS. A VERY BASIC NUDE. LIKE WHAT YOU MIGHT FIND IN A PUBLIC BATHROOM. THIS MAKES THE ARTIST STOP AND SO DOES THE MODEL. SHE SLOWLY CLOSES THE BOOK AND TOSSES IT ONTO A COUNTER.

ARTIST   Does that make you feel good--doing that to me? (BEAT) Hmmm?

MODEL   Not at all.

ARTIST   No?

MODEL   Uh-huh. Makes me sick, actually. I feel like throwing up...

ARTIST   Great. My best review yet...

MODEL   Not about the 'art.' Jesus...about you lying to me, like that. For so long...

ARTIST   'Lying?' What does that even mean?

MODEL   You know.

ARTIST   No, I don't...I really don't.

MODEL   Just say it to me--one time--and I will go and we'll be done with it. Just once. (BEAT) Can you do that?

ARTIST   What?

MODEL   Say it...what you've done...

ARTIST   This is...so...! Ahh! Frustrating!!

MODEL   Say it to me...what you've been doing here. What this is...

ARTIST   'This' relaxes me. It's my hobby.

MODEL That's not what I asked.

ARTIST It is, though...

MODEL That part I believe. It's your hobby.

ARTIST It is!

MODEL I-BELIEVE-YOU.

SHE MOVES AWAY FROM THE ARTIST. THE ARTIST DOESN'T UNDERSTAND SO SHE SHRUGS AND WATCHES HER.

MODEL Okay? I believe you do this on your free time and that you enjoy it... (BEAT) But paying people to stare at them naked...to check out their tits and cocks, all the shit you've done...that's your hobby, not drawing...I know I'm right! I know it!!

ARTIST ...that's not...

MODEL Please! I can see now what you've been doing here! I can, and I don't need to be some PhD in fucking...whatever...Art History stuff...to know the truth of it. (BEAT) You've been paying me to stare at me. My body. My pussy. Just say it to me. (BEAT) Please. (BEAT) Say it and I'll walk away. No harm, no foul.

ARTIST ...fine.

MODEL Is that a 'yes?'

ARTIST If it gets you to leave, then fine. (BEAT) Yes.

MODEL You have?

ARTIST Stop!

MODEL I'm asking if...you're...

ARTIST I already said it! I just did! Yes, that's what I've been doing...yes, you're so smart...you figured me out...now please leave my house.

MODEL Alright. I will.

ARTIST Good. Thank you.

MODEL   But you won't just say...

ARTIST   I said it! Yes! It's true! YES!

MODEL   But...is it? (BEAT) Is it?

ARTIST   I don't know! You the smart one, you figure it out...

MODEL   Just tell me! You're not saying it like you mean it...so...that's...

ARTIST   Now I don't tell the truth right! Jesus, I mean...wow. First I'm a liar and then...no. No. First I'm not an artist or, or, what? A bad artist...an awful artist...

MODEL   I said that you're...no, I said...

ARTIST   Which is possible, by the way...to be just a bad artist, which I have said that I am; I never claimed to be great or even good...but then, no, that's not enough...you're saying that I'm not any kind of artist and just doing this to look at you naked--which I could do for a hell of a lot less money at a strip club but that doesn't matter apparently, that's not even factored in here--I could just go down to that damn place over on tenth...what's it called, Peppermint-something? With the neon lady out front? I can go in there for a few dollars and get food and everything, see all kinds of naked women...and yes, including the 'pussy,' as you so gently call it, any day of the week...

MODEL   Women don't go to strip clubs that much, though...

ARTIST   That's not true!

MODEL   Yeah, kinda...

ARTIST   No, it's not! They do all the time. With their boyfriends and alone... I could easily do that if I wanted. But no, instead I've built up some elaborate game with you because you must be the most amazing MODEL in the world, you must have the most golden 'pussy' of them all...the seventh wonder of, of puss-ies or whatnot...that must be it...that makes a lot more sense than just the fact that I've struck a deal with you and it was all fine and good but you had to do something that I asked you not to do--the ONE thing that I asked--and so here we are...you calling me names and saying all sorts of terrible shit about me and my talents. (THROWS HER ARMS UP) I KNOW I'm not talented! I KNOW that!

I am not gifted. You could've just asked me, I would've said the same thing...but no, you had to get all Lot's wife on me and make the bad shit happen. So fine... turn into salt, see if I care. (BEAT) Just go away, please. Go away now...

THE MODEL STANDS THERE FOR A MOMENT, TAKING ALL THIS IN. THE ARTIST MAKES A PRETTY GOOD CASE FOR HERSELF.

MODEL   What's Lot's wife? I don't get it.

ARTIST   From The Bible. It's a biblical reference. (BEAT) Old Testament.

MODEL   Oh.

ARTIST   Yeah. It was this guy's wife...

MODEL   "Lot?"

ARTIST   Yes...his wife. She got turned into a pillar of salt. For being bad...

MODEL   'Bad?'

ARTIST   Or doing a 'bad' thing! Something like that...! What she was asked not to do...she looked back on a place that she had no business to be looking back on--Sodom or one of those cities--and so that's what came of that... (BEAT) And got left, too, because she just couldn't do what God asked her to do...and if it wasn't God then it was somebody else of equal importance. A god-like presence. Not just her husband--it was God. Okay? GOD said it...and she still couldn't listen... (BEAT) Anyhow, I think you oughta go now and consider all I've said and...just...see how it works out for you in the end. (BEAT) I have another model.

MODEL   Right. That's true...

ARTIST   I can see if he's free Saturdays.

MODEL   Yep...then you can spend an hour staring at him naked...

ARTIST   STOP IT! Stop saying that shit! I am an artist and I enjoy working with live models, okay? I do not care what you think of me or my work...just go away! GET OUT!!

MODEL   I'm going!

ARTIST   Then do it!! GO!!

MODEL   I AM!! (BEAT) ...but I'll tell you what...you don't do what you do for years and years and not progress...that much I know. You get better. It's not just an 'art,' it's also a 'craft' and like anything else-- sewing or sculpting or whatever-- YOU GET BETTER. If you were really spending your time drawing me, over and over and over, for all of these months...you'd see it in the pages of those books. It would be obvious and there's no way around it. There isn't. (POINTS) The proof is there.

ARTIST   Bullshit...

MODEL   Call it whatever you want, but...

ARTIST   I am. I'm saying it right now...

MODEL   Yeah? Tell me...what is it you're actually saying? Tell me. Go on...

ARTIST   I'm a mediocre artist...a hack...

MODEL   ...

ARTIST   ...I'll never be any good at it but you know what? I adhere to a school of art, a movement that is abstract and it's not everybody's cup of tea and... so what? So-what? I shouldn't do it, practice it, just because it doesn't create pretty pictures? Is that what you think? 'Cubism' came out of that school...and 'Abstract Expressionism.' It's not for everybody but I love it. I do. And that is the art I make...even if it's a lousy, not-very-talented version of it. That's what I enjoy doing and I don't think it's hurting anybody. It's just like my music. I'm not a musician, but I buy music all the time. Itunes. Dozens and dozens of albums... I'm thinking of renting a piano and guess what? If I do...if I go in the shop and I ask to rent one? They'll do it. They will not ask me how good I am...or say I must be better by so-and-so date. No. Never. That will not happen. They will ask for my credit card and be amazed that they were still able to rent a piano in this day and age and that'll be the end of it...do you understand me?

MODEL   ...I think so...

ARTIST   No tests along the way...neighbors upstairs or down won't be able to come to me in January and say 'you should be playing Mozart by now so you have to stop practicing.' It'll be mine to do as I see fit, whether I ever get one bit better at it or not... (BEAT) That's the beauty of art. It is subjective. It is not a race. I don't have to win to do it. Loving it is enough. Wanting to be an artist is enough. I don't have to have any other reason than that. Not for you...not for anybody...I don't. I'm an artist because I say I am. It's that simple.

MODEL   Fine. (BEAT) Then...fine...

ARTIST   Yeah. Fine. (BEAT) And another thing:

MODEL   What?

ARTIST   IF I was doing that...

MODEL   ...what...?

ARTIST   If I was doing what you said--paying you money to stare at your beautiful body--which you do have, by the way, without question, it's spectacular-- IF I was doing that very thing...sitting over there in my chair for sixty minutes per session and over-paying you for the priviledge...would it be such a terrible thing? Hmmmmm? Would it really be so, so awful...?

MODEL   I mean...yes. I wouldn't like it.

ARTIST   No?

MODEL   No. I personally wouldn't wanna be a part of that...

ARTIST   I see. Because...of...?

MODEL   It'd make me feel gross. And cheap. Being used that way...

ARTIST   Like a whore?

THAT WORD LANDS HARD--THE MODEL LOOKS OVER AT THE ARTIST.

MODEL   Yeah. Kinda.

ARTIST   You mean...as if you were selling your body for a little money?

MODEL   I guess so...

ARTIST   Which...I'm sorry...isn't that what you're doing now? Have been doing? (BEAT) I'm just asking...

MODEL   For...yes, but for a whole other reason...! A big big difference!

ARTIST   How so?

MODEL   Because! It...was for...'art.'

ARTIST   Really.

MODEL   Yes! Among other things...yeah.

ARTIST   And that's why you came here...to be a part of making 'art?'

MODEL   That's a lot of it...no question.

ARTIST   With someone who told you from the very beginning that they never displayed their work...never showed it to anyone...or put it in public...? Was that the kind of art you were hoping to be involved with, because I thought you were here for money--

MODEL   Yeah, but...

ARTIST   I thought you answered my ad looking for a job...since you asked me what it paid, first thing you said--

MODEL   Modeling for an artist is a lot different than spreading your legs for some man or woman just so they can stare at you--I mean, come on!

ARTIST   I guess so.

MODEL   Course it is! Please! Job or not...

ARTIST   Fine. If it is, then fine...

MODEL   You don't think so? Really?

ARTIST   I think you do something and then you get paid. (BEAT) I think it's actually as easy as that.

MODEL   ...

ARTIST   You choose to take off your clothes and you get fifty dollars at the end...the rest is semantics.

MODEL   Wow.

ARTIST   It's just an opinion. Mine. Can I not have that now, either...or...?

MODEL   Sure, go on, have it...I just think you're full of shit, that's all.

ARTIST   You think I'm a terrible artist...that's even worse.

MODEL   You are bad.

ARTIST   I know it.

MODEL   You know it? You're aware of it?

ARTIST   I mean...I'd have to be a TERRIBLE artist if I didn't look down at my pages...all those pages...and not know that. (BEAT) Of course I am. (BEAT) But you're wrong about the rest...I am trying to get better. I'm just very bad and very slow at making progress...but I am trying. Every time we get together, I am trying to further my technique...trying to advance my shadowing...whether you can see it or not.

MODEL   Well...it makes me uncomfortable. Knowing what I know now...feeling the way I do...

ARTIST   Good art should make you uncomfortable...that's what it's for.

MODEL   Is that right?

ARTIST   I think so...yes.

MODEL   And so...what about your art?

ARTIST   That apparently makes you uncomfortable for other reasons...

MODEL   (WITH IRONY) Yeah.

ARTIST   And so...here we are...

MODEL   Guess so. (BEAT) Anyway...

ARTIST   Just so you know...I have never and will never pay you or someone else to simply come here so I can stare at their...you know...their bits...

MODEL   If you say so.

ARTIST   Much much easier to go to a bar and pick up a drunk...bring 'em back here and sketch 'em as they sleep it off...

THE ARTIST SHRUGS AT THIS--THE TRUTH. THE MODEL TAKES IT IN.

MODEL   I see. (BEAT) Well, I think things here are kinda ruined now, so...

ARTIST   Only if you make it that way.

MODEL   Yeah, but...I don't feel like I can really trust you again...so...

ARTIST   Trust *me*? Because...of...?

MODEL   You know.

ARTIST   No...what did I do? I mean...really do? To you? (BEAT) You just blurted shit out about me...true or not...you're the one who started this...by looking through all my things!

MODEL   Just...

ARTIST   But I can try again...if you can...

MODEL   Yeah?

ARTIST   Yes. (BEAT) I could probably even pay a little bit more...maybe...

MODEL   I think it'll feel weird...

ARTIST   Of course...but we can do it slowly...just try it once or twice...

MODEL   ...

ARTIST   I felt very comfortable with you...that's why I used you so much, way more than the guy I've had over a few times. (BEAT) I think that we connect... in a lot of ways...

MODEL   Yeah. I guess.

ARTIST   Well, I'm just saying, from my side of things...I'm willing to give it a go again. (BEAT) From scratch.

MODEL   That's...

ARTIST   Up to you, I'm just saying from my point of view...I'm willing to do that. (BEAT) Take it or leave it. (BEAT) I'm just offering...

THE ARTIST STOPS AND LET'S THE MODEL THINK ABOUT THIS. THE MODEL LOOKS AT THE OLDER WOMAN, CONSIDERING ALL THAT SHE'S SAID.

MODEL   I don't think I can. (BEAT) You've never been on the other side of it, so...that's...

ARTIST   No, I haven't...

MODEL   Right...you don't know what it can feel like...opening up like that to a person...physically and...just...all of it. And I have body issues, too, so...shit from when I was a kid... (BEAT) It's not easy.

ARTIST   I know. I do know.

MODEL   No, you don't.

ARTIST   No, but I mean, what it must feel like...to do that. To trust someone like that...completely...when you've been...

MODEL   I mean, you said yourself that you couldn't do it...so...

ARTIST   I couldn't. But I can empathize...I can imagine how hard it is to give yourself over to something like that...

MODEL   Maybe.

ARTIST   I can!

MODEL   Maybe so...but I'd feel a lot more safe...a lot more like you really do know what I mean if you'd done it, too...somehow...

ARTIST   Yes...I mean, I can see where that might be true...but...

MODEL   Yeah.

THE MODEL IS STARING AT THE ARTIST. THE ARTIST IS TRYING TO READ THE MOMENT. SHE OFFERS HER HAND. THE MODEL TAKES IT.

ARTIST   So...then...are we...what...?

MODEL   Yes. We can try again. I guess.

ARTIST   Oh, good...that's excellent! I'm so pleased! Thank you!

MODEL   Yeah, we can...I mean...IF.

ARTIST   Hmmmm?

THE ARTIST TURNS TO THE MODEL. SHE IS STARING STRAIGHT AT HER. A MOMENT OF SILENCE.

MODEL   IF you do that...what you just talked about.

ARTIST   I don't understand.

MODEL   I'm saying I'll go back to being your model...for another twenty-five dollars an hour...

ARTIST   Oh. (BEAT) I see.

MODEL   I think I'll feel better about it, coming over here, if you pay me a bit more...not a lot but just a little bit more...since I still think that maybe you do it for...you know...some other reasons. Other than your...'art.'

ARTIST   Fine. (BEAT) So it is about money, then.

MODEL   No...not just...no.

ARTIST   But that's part of it--the money thing is part of all this. It is.

MODEL   Ok, fine. A little bit. Yes.

ARTIST   Alright then. (BEAT) I'll pay.

MODEL   Yes?

ARTIST   Yes. Seventy-five is fine.

MODEL   Ok. I mean...you brought it up... (BEAT) And the other thing, too.

ARTIST   Sorry?

MODEL   I need you to know what it's like, if I'm going to keep putting myself out there for you...I need that.

ARTIST   ...so...I...what does that mean?

MODEL   I wanna draw you right now. (BEAT) Naked. (BEAT) That's what I want.

ARTIST   That's absurd. Come on...what...?

MODEL   It's up to you.

ARTIST   Well...'no,' then. If it's up to me.

MODEL   Fine. Ok...but I won't be back.

THE MODEL HEADS TOWARD THE DOOR. THE ARTIST STOPS HER ONLY AT THE LAST MOMENT.

ARTIST   Ahhhhhhhhh! (BEAT) For how long...?

MODEL   An hour.

ARTIST   But...

MODEL   One session.

ARTIST   ...

MODEL   Your choice.

ARTIST   That's--and will you pay me? After?

MODEL   (SMILING AT THIS) Sure. Thirty bucks...for beginners.

THE ARTIST TAKES THIS IN, APPRECIATING THE IRONY OF IT.

ARTIST   Seems fair.

MODEL   Ok. (BEAT) Let's get started then.

ARTIST   (UNBUTTONING HER DRESS) I'm not...look, just so you know...I get why you're doing this, I do, but I REALLY don't wanna sit for you...

MODEL   I know you don't...and that's why you should.

ARTIST   No, but I mean...I really really don't want to. (BEAT) *Please*.

MODEL   Totally up to you...

THE MODEL GOES TO THE CHAIR. PICKS UP THE PAD. SITS. WAITS. THE ART-IST THINKS ABOUT IT FOR A LONG MOMENT, THEN SLOWLY REMOVES HER CLOTHES AND SITS IN FRONT OF THE MODEL.

MODEL   ...now...open up a bit. To me. Turn and open up...no, I don't mean just twist. I mean your legs. Open up.

THE ARTIST DOES AS SHE'S TOLD. HER LEGS SLOWLY SPREAD OPEN.

MODEL   That's it. (BEAT) Wider. (BEAT) Wider. (BEAT) Just a bit...wider.

THE ARTIST STOPS FOR A BEAT, TAKES A DEEP BREATH, THEN OBEYS.

MODEL   ...that's lovely.

ARTIST   Thank you.

THE MODEL BEGINS TO SKETCH HER SUBJECT, THEN STOPS. SHE GETS UP, CROSSES AND SETS THE EGG TIMER. IT BEGINS TO TICK. SHE RETURNS TO HER CHAIR AND TO HER WORK. STARTS TO SKETCH AGAIN. A DARK TRIANGLE BEGINNING TO APPEAR ON THE PAGE. HER SUBJECT TURNS AND STARES OFF. DIRECTLY AT THE AUDIENCE.

HATE CRIME

HATE CRIME had its world premiere at the Gaslight Theater as part of the 'LaBute New Theater Festival' in St. Louis Missouri in July 2017 and subsequently at the 59E59 street theaters in New York as part of the 'NYC LaBute New Theater Festival' in January 2018. Both were directed by John Pierson.

Man 1: Chauncy Thomas   Man 2: Greg Hunsaker (Spencer Sickmann – NYC)

(left to right) Chauncy Thomas , Greg Hunsaker
Photo: Patrick Huber

A ROOM SOMEWHERE. LOOKS LIKE IT'S A HOTEL ROOM OR ONE THAT'S BEEN FURNISHED CARELESSLY. DOESN'T FEEL LIKE A HOME. A MAN SITS IN A CHAIR. WATCHING A TV. IN THE DARK. SEEMS LIKE A REGULAR GUY. REGULAR-LOOKING. REGULAR-BUILD. YOU KNOW THE TYPE. 'REGULAR.' AFTER A MOMENT, A KNOCK AT THE DOOR. THE MAN DOESN'T MOVE. KEEPS WATCHING HIS SHOW. ANOTHER KNOCK AND HE FINALLY GETS UP. CROSSES TO THE DOOR. OPENS IT. ANOTHER MAN STEPS IN. NICE-LOOKING. ANYTHING BUT 'REGULAR.' THEY KISS BRIEFLY. HE CARRIES A BAG AND TWO COFFEES. DROPS THESE ON A COUNTER AND GOES TO A TABLE. SITS.

MAN 1   ...hey.

MAN 2   Hey. (BEAT) Where's your key?

MAN 1   I dunno...I left it here, I guess, or something. I don't have it, so... I must've left it here. (BEAT) Last time, or...maybe...?

MAN 2   I haven't seen it.

MAN 1   No?

MAN 2   Uh-huh. And I'm always here...

MAN 1   Oh. (BEAT) That's weird.

MAN 2   Yeah, you didn't leave it here, so I hope you've got it somewhere... in your car or some place.

MAN 1   Probably so.

MAN 2   You wanna check?

MAN 1   I will.

MAN 2   You should do that. Do it now...before you forget.

MAN 1   I will.

MAN 2   But I mean...like...'right' now.

MAN 1   I'm gonna. In just a minute.

MAN 2   Okay. But soon.

MAN 1   I will. I just need a second… (BEAT) I mean, I just walked in and it's hot outside. (BEAT) Ok?

MAN 2   I know it's not here…

MAN 1   Yeah, I know. You said that.

MAN 2   And if you don't have it…

MAN 1   I don't *think* I have it. Maybe I do, out in the car or shoved in a pocket or something…

MAN 2   That's pretty casual for something so valuable.

MAN 1   I'm just saying…

MAN 2   I know, but…you need to hear what I'm saying right now…that key is very very important. Okay? It is. (MORE) And it probably looks just like the other one…the one from your other room…they all look the same these days, keys for hotel rooms…

MAN 1   I know.

MAN 2   Yeah, you know, but suddenly you set this one down, the one for the door here to this room, and you're just going about your day and you put it down on the table or some chest of drawers next to the lamp and somebody sees that…sees that you have a key to some other hotel room…a hotel room that they know nothing about and suddenly…guess what…?

MAN 1   What?

MAN 2   We've got a problem.

MAN 1   I understand.

MAN 2   Okay, good, because that would be a real big problem…one that we just might not overcome. (BEAT) That's all I'm gonna say…so maybe you can check your pockets now and your car…right this instant…just so my stomach isn't tying itself in knots…can you do that for me?

MAN 1 LOOKS AT MAN 2, THEN CROSSES TO HIS COAT. DIGS AROUND IN THE

POCKETS. NOTHING. STANDS UP. GOES THROUGH HIS PANTS POCKETS. NOTHING.

MAN 1 I know I've got it...

MAN 2 Hope so. Hope you didn't leave it somewhere...on a counter when you were buying those coffees and the whatever-you-got-theres... (SHOWS HIM) Some kinda pastries.

MAN 1 Danish.

MAN 1 KEEPS SEARCHING WHILE THEY TALK BACK AND FORTH.

MAN 2 Danish pastries?

MAN 1 Yes.

MAN 2 Like...from Denmark?

MAN 1 No. God. I bought Danish. Danish are pastries. (BEAT) Aren't they?

MAN 2 I guess so...yeah. I think so.

MAN 1 Yeah. Me, too.

MAN 2 Actually, I dunno. Are they?

MAN 1 I'm pretty sure.

MAN 2 Okay, then, they probably are. I mean, if you think they are...if you've seen that before, on some sign or whatever...then they no doubt are called that. 'Danish.'

MAN 1 But not all of 'em.

MAN 2 Huh?

MAN 1 Not all of them are Danishes.

MAN 2 Oh. (BEAT) They're not?

MAN 1 No. Not all pastries are Danishes but these are. With the fruit in the center...or some cheese. Like this one... (HE SHOWS MAN 2) That's a 'cheese' Danish. (BEAT) See?

MAN 1 PULLS ANOTHER ONE OUT OF THE BAG. THIS ONE HAS CHEESE AND FRUIT. MAN 2 GLANCES OVER AT IT.

MAN 2   That doesn't look like cheese.

MAN 1   It's not. I mean...not like a regular type of cheese, like a cheddar or that kind of thing. This is more of a sweeter type. A sweet cheese. (BEAT) Soft.

MAN 2   Oh.

MAN 1   Yeah. (BEAT) Anyway, I brought you breakfast. Figured you could use some...

MAN 2   Thanks. Coffee's great...and I'll try the other thing there...this pastry thing. The Danish.

MAN 1   Good. (FEELS ANOTHER POCKET) Ahhh! Look...

HE REACHES IN AND PULLS OUT A HOTEL PASS KEY. PLASTIC. HE SHOWS IT TO MAN 2.

MAN 2   Your key.

MAN 1   Yep.

MAN 2   You had it.

MAN 1   I did. The whole time...

MAN 2   But up there. In your shirt pocket. Right where somebody could find it. (BEAT) That's not great.

MAN 1   Sorry.

MAN 2   That's still a bit dangerous...

MAN 1   Sorry.

MAN 2   That's the kind of thing that I was talking about--kind of mistake that puts an end to the whole thing that we're doing here...our plans.

MAN 1   I said 'I'm sorry.' (BEAT) It won't happen again.

MAN 2   Okay.

MAN 1 Okay?

MAN 2 It's fine.

MAN 1 No, it's not.

MAN 2 I mean...

MAN 1 I know it's not and I'm sorry and I won't do it again. I promise.

MAN 2 Okay.

MAN 1 Okay. (BEAT) I should go. It's time for me to start getting back...

MAN 2 Yeah. You should.

MAN 1 Yeah. I have to.

MAN 2 I don't want you to...but...

MAN 1 I get it.

MAN 2 But you should.

MAN 1 Right. I said I'd be back so I need to do it.

MAN 2 I'd rather you stayed here...if it were up to me, I'd have you stay right here with me...

MAN 1 I'd like that.

MAN 2 Yeah?

MAN 1 Yes.

MAN 2 Why's that?

MAN 1 Because I like you...

MAN 2 Yeah?

MAN 1 Yes.

MAN 2 You 'like' me.

MAN 1 I do. I like you. A lot.

MAN 2 That sounds nice...when you say it like that. All...soft...like that.

MAN 1 It's meant to.

MAN 2 Well, it does.

MAN 1 Good.

MAN 2 And a little bit dirty, too. At the same time.

MAN 1 It's meant to sound that way, too.

MAN 2 Yeah?

MAN 1 Yes.

MAN 2 Well...it does. It sounds dirty.

MAN 1 Good.

MAN 1 STANDS THERE. MAN 2 JUST STARES AT HIM. SILENT.

MAN 1) He thinks I went for a run...

MAN 2 Oh.

MAN 1 So I've still got a little time, but I need to get all sweaty and that sorta thing, too...so...

MAN 2 I can help you with that...

MAN 1 I bet you could.

MAN 2 I really could.

MAN 1 I like the sound of that...like the sound of that a lot.

MAN 2 Do you?

MAN 1 You know I do.

MAN 2 Well, then...

MAN 1 But we can't...

MAN 2 No?

MAN 1 You know we can't. I can't have a trace of you on me...not anywhere on me...not for a few weeks. (BEAT) You know that.

MAN 2 I know.

MAN 1 Of course you do...I'm just saying it again to remind us. Both.

MAN 2 You don't have to remind me...

MAN 1 I'm sure.

MAN 2 It's part of the plan.

MAN 1 That's right.

MAN 2 Part of the plan we made.

MAN 1 Together.

MAN 2 That's right.

MAN 1 And we're doing it...right now.

MAN 2 Yep. Very soon.

MAN 1 Very.

MAN 2 Un-huh.

MAN 1 Right after the wedding.

MAN 2 Immediately after.

MAN 1 That's right.

MAN 2 Which makes sense...

MAN 1 It does. It absolutely does.

MAN 2 I know.

MAN 1 I know you do…I'm just saying…

MAN 2 What?

MAN 1 I'm agreeing with you. That's what we said we'd do and it's the best idea we've had…

MAN 2 It is.

MAN 1 Because no one's ever gonna expect it, right?

MAN 2 That's right.

MAN 1 The same day I get married is the same day that my partner dies… nobody would ever suspect a thing like that. (BEAT) Would they?

MAN 2 I wouldn't.

MAN 1 Me, either.

MAN 2 And I don't think anybody would… (BEAT) That's just not…if someone said they did, that they figured it out or that we'd made a mistake doing it that way…I wouldn't believe 'em. (BEAT) I really wouldn't.

MAN 1 And so that's why we're doing it.

MAN 2 Exactly.

MAN 1 I mean, it's supposed to be…you know…like the happiest day of your life…of your entire life. Your wedding day. And nowadays, now that anybody can marry anybody, any man or woman can marry some other man or woman…now that everyone can experience that same sort of happiness…it's kinda perfect.

MAN 2 True…

MAN 1 And so if some man goes and gets married to another man that he loves…some man he met not long ago but long enough for them to be a couple… long enough for people to get to know them in their new neighborhood and to think that they make a very sweet pair…the older one and the pretty one; that's what they call 'em sometimes, when they see 'em together or out at dinner. 'The older one and the pretty one.'

MAN 2   I'm guessing you're the 'pretty' one.

MAN 1   Ha! Thank you...

MAN 2   Am I right?

MAN 1   Yes.

MAN 2   Yeah? I figured I was...

MAN 1   You are. You are absolutely smack dab on the money...

MAN 2   Thought so.

MAN 1   And so...if this older one decides that this is what he wants, to be married to this pretty one...very pretty for such a plain and older man like he is...if he were to ask the pretty one to marry him...tell him that he'll always make him happy and feel safe and, and loved...tells him that he will forever make him financially well off and secure...and so then they go to get married but before they do...even before they plan a ceremony and all that other business...even before that they each take out these, like...big policies on each other...these two very large life insurance policies...

MAN 2   Huh. (BEAT) They do, huh?

MAN 1   Yes, they do...

MAN 2   Well, that's okay.

MAN 1   It is. Absolutely okay.

MAN 2   It's perfectly legal to do so.

MAN 1   That's true.

MAN 2   People do it all the time...

MAN 1   Every day of the week.

MAN 2   Right. Especially loved ones.

MAN 1   And so that's what they do. They do that same thing. Just in case...for a rainy day, they say to each other with big smiles on their faces. Big policies and big smiles.

MAN 2   How big?

MAN 1   Pretty big...very very good size...many dollars worth. That's how big. Hundreds of thousands of dollars worth...

MAN 2   Interesting.

MAN 1   It is interesting, isn't it? That they would both have those...these massive policies on their lives...and even though they'll be married very soon... and virtually on the same day as the older man dies...

MAN 2   Because he's murdered...

MAN 1   That's right--even though he's killed in cold blood--on his way home from the store in what looks like some sort of...attack...

MAN 2   Not a hit-and-run, though.

MAN 1   No. Not that.

MAN 2   But not a mugging, either.

MAN 1   No. (BEAT) His wallet is still there. There on the ground...

MAN 2   At the scene of the crime.

MAN 1   No money was taken.

MAN 2   He was just killed.

MAN 1   For no reason...

MAN 2   Well...no...not 'no' reason...nobody gets killed for 'no reason.' It doesn't just happen.

MAN 1   Sometimes it does...

MAN 2 THINKS ABOUT THIS FOR A BEAT, THEN SHAKES HIS HEAD.

MAN 2   ...no...

MAN 1   Sure it does.

MAN 2   Like when?

MAN 1   Someone...I dunno...walks out into traffic...or...or...

MAN 2   Then they did that. They walked out there, into traffic...even by mistake, they did that...

MAN 1   Okay, alright...or a piece of some building falls down...or one of the big...you know...cranes they have up there in the air, lifting stuff, one of those comes crashing down...people do just die sometimes...

MAN 2   ...okay...but...

MAN 1   That's a 'no reason.' Isn't it? No reason for that to happen...

MAN 2   Well...maybe...

MAN 1   I mean, more so than this. What we're doing here...

MAN 2   That's true.

MAN 1   That's all I'm saying...

MAN 2   This is more calculated.

MAN 1   Planned.

MAN 2   That's right. This is something we talked about...for some time now...

MAN 1   Very true.

MAN 2   And so, yeah...he dies. This man.

MAN 1   On the street.

MAN 2   In the alley, actually. I'm gonna do it in that alley I told you about...

MAN 1   That's right. (BEAT) Behind the store.

MAN 2   That's the one. The 'short-cut.'

MAN 1   Where it's dark.

MAN 2   And quiet.

MAN 1 And no one can see you.

MAN 2 That's right.

MAN 1 That's where he'll die...where you're gonna take his life.

MAN 2 It'll be a 'hate' crime.

MAN 1 That's true. That's what it's gonna look like...

MAN 2 'Cause you can tell he's gay...

MAN 1 That's right.

MAN 2 From how he looks...

MAN 1 Uh-huh.

MAN 2 His earring...

MAN 1 Yeah...

MAN 2 In the right ear.

MAN 1 I see.

MAN 2 Like a gay man wears it.

MAN 1 Sure.

MAN 2 Or a man who is gay but hasn't let himself go yet...married and kids and all that shit...but deep in his heart he's gay. Lots of people do that, in their lives...go around being secretly gay and unhappy. With their little earrings... and, you know...dressing all perfect, with crisp new chinos. Yeah.

MAN 1 True.

MAN 2 Or the glasses that he chooses to wear...they'll be some color...

MAN 1 Like red.

MAN 2 Right, red. That's gay. Or...the style that a lot of gay guys would choose...

MAN 1 That's true.

MAN 2   Thick frames.

MAN 1   In fashion...

MAN 2   Sure.

MAN 1   And expensive.

MAN 2   Yep...of course they are.

MAN 1   You should crush those glasses.

MAN 2   I plan to...

MAN 1   When you do it. When you kill him.

MAN 2   I'm gonna do that. Step right on 'em and crush 'em into the dirt...

MAN 1   Good.

MAN 2   Yeah? You want me to do that?

MAN 1   I do.

MAN 2   Okay. (BEAT) Okay, I will then.

MAN 1 THINKS ABOUT THIS FOR A MOMENT, THEN TOSSES A THOUGHT OUT THERE FOR MAN 2:

MAN 1   I hate the...you know...the feel of 'em...against my face...when he's kissing me. His glasses.

MAN 2   Yeah. I can see that.

MAN 1   The way they push up against my face when he's right here...up here...close to my mouth...and kissing me. I hate that.

MAN 2   I can imagine.

MAN 1   And his tongue...

MAN 2   I'll bet he does that a lot. Puts his tongue in your mouth...

MAN 1   He does.

MAN 2 That's disgusting...

MAN 1 He kisses too hard.

MAN 2 And you don't like it...

MAN 1 No.

MAN 2 I understand. (BEAT) Do you like the way that I kiss you?

MAN 1 Yeah, I do.

MAN 2 Just like a man's supposed to kiss, right? Tender but firm.

MAN 1 I think so.

MAN 2 Strong...

MAN 1 Yes. Very.

MAN 2 ...but not hard. Not hard all the time...like I've got something to prove.

MAN 1 Exactly.

MAN 2 There's a difference.

MAN 1 There absolutely is. (BEAT) You want a Danish? With your coffee?

MAN 2 Yeah, I'll take a little bit of one...maybe the fruit. Not that 'cheese' one.

MAN 1 Cheese is good, though...

MAN 2 Yeah, but that's...some other time, maybe. I'll try the 'cheese.'

MAN 1 Okay.

MAN 2 TURNS BACK TO THE TV WHILE MAN 1 CUTS HIM A PIECE. HE THEN BRINGS IT TO HIM. BEFORE MAN 2 TAKES THE PLATE HE PUTS HIS HANDS ON MAN 1. RUBS THEM ACROSS HIS BODY AND UP, PULLING MAN 1 CLOSER TO HIMSELF.

MAN 1 Careful now...I can't have any of you on me...you know that...

MAN 2 I know...I know...

MAN 1 I'm sorry about that, but I can't.

MAN 2 I know you can't. I know the plan. (BEAT) I *made* the plan...

MAN 1 Okay then...

MAN 2 Okay.

MAN 2 TAKES THE PLATE AND MAN 1 MOVES AWAY. SITS DOWN AND WAITS WHILE MAN 2 TRIES THE PASTRY. HE SEEMS TO LIKE IT.

MAN 1 You decide how you're gonna do it yet?

MAN 2 What?

MAN 1 You know...do it...with him?

MAN 2 Oh. That.

MAN 1 Yeah. 'That.'

MAN 2 I mean, I guess...

MAN 1 Yeah, so 'how?'

MAN 2 Just...beat him, I think...

MAN 1 Yeah?

MAN 2 I think so.

MAN 1 Okay.

MAN 2 It's probably the easiest...and it's the most like, you know...the way people do...when people die that way. In a hate crime...a lot of times it's a beating.

MAN 1 What way?

MAN 2 Die just because they're hated. Because somebody hates who they are or...what they are...things they stand for...you know what I mean. (BEAT) Hate crimes...when those people die, a lot of times they just get beat.

MAN 1 Sure.

MAN 2 Most times when you read about those...the people got beaten to death. Right? Isn't that true?

MAN 1 I guess so. Yeah.

MAN 2 I think so. I mean, on average.

MAN 1 Okay.

MAN 2 Sometimes it's different...they'll get shot or, maybe stabbed or something like that...that guy who killed those folks in San Francisco a few years back...however long ago now...we watched the movie about it together... remember that?

MAN 1 Ummmm...

MAN 2 With the other guy...the good actor guy...he was in it...

MAN 1 I don't remember now...

MAN 2 You know who I mean...he's really good...in a lot of stuff...

MAN 1 Yeah, but I don't know his name.

MAN 2 That one guy. The *actor*.

MAN 1 ...ummmmm...

MAN 2 He's literally been in a hundred movies. (BEAT) THE THIN RED LINE.

MAN 1 That was all guys! The whole movie. (BEAT) Which one was he?

MAN 2 I dunno...with the machine gun...

MAN 1 Seriously?

MAN 2 Well, anyway, they all got shot. At least two of 'em...the mayor and... and the other guy...that actor we both like...in the gay movie.

MAN 1 ...okay...

MAN 2 But usually it's a beating or that type of thing. So that's what I'm gonna do...I'm just gonna beat the fuck outta your husband and leave him for dead...

MAN 1 Good. (BEAT) But...not...

MAN 2   What?

MAN 1   Not 'for' dead...not just that...

MAN 2   No. 'Course not.

MAN 1   Okay.

MAN 2   He's gonna be actually dead. Like 'dead' dead.

MAN 1   Right. That's what I mean...

MAN 2   Nothing to chance.

MAN 1   Good.

MAN 2   I'm gonna jump out the bushes there on the path...where it narrows...

MAN 1   Because in the lobby, I'm gonna ask him to go get me some candy or something like that...*condoms*...and tell him to take the 'short-cut.

MAN 2   Right...in front of the concierge or somebody...so that one of the employees there hears you. Hears the whole thing...

MAN 1   ...right...

MAN 2   About what you ask for and where he's going and that you're gonna go wait for him...make a big deal about it...OR waiting in the bar. A public place... even better.

MAN 1   Before we go watch the fireworks down on the beach...later...

MAN 2   That's right. That's exactly the story...a romantic story.

MAN 1   But instead...

MAN 2   Yeah...instead I'm gonna be there, waiting for him...on the path...and then I'm gonna grab something out there...a brick or a rock, or, or...I dunno...a piece of pipe I find out there and I'm gonna beat the living shit outta him. I will beat his ugly little faggot face in until it's nothing but a pile of mush...that's what I'm gonna do.

MAN 1   Alright.

MAN 2   Yeah. Alright.

MAN 1   And then...oh, and I'll make sure he's wearing his PRIDE shirt...that rainbow-looking one that he likes so much...I'll be sure he's got that on, too...

MAN 2   That's good. Yeah. Perfect.

MAN 1   And then...what else?

MAN 2   We wait.

MAN 1   Okay.

MAN 2   We wait and wait and listen and wait until the insurance company sniffs around and asks all their questions and analyzes the shit outta things and talks to you and his friends and you again and to the hotel clerk and whoever the hell else they wanna talk to...we wait months if we have to... (BEAT) You got that? Months.

MAN 1   I understand.

MAN 2   Yeah?

MAN 1   Yes. (BEAT) We wait however long it takes...to get that check.

MAN 2   So: you think you can do that?

MAN 1   Yes.

MAN 2   Yeah?

MAN 1   Yes.

MAN 2   You sure?

MAN 1   Yeah. I can. (BEAT) Totally.

MAN 2   And you can live with that...with what we've done...what we're about to do to this guy?

MAN 1   I think so.

MAN 2   No. That's not... (BEAT) NO.

MAN 1 What?

MAN 2 Not 'think' so. I don't wanna hear that...at all...

MAN 1 Okay. (BEAT) I know so.

MAN 2 That's better...

MAN 1 I know I can.

MAN 2 That's what I like to hear.

MAN 1 So let's do it then...

MAN 2 We're gonna. We're doing it. (BEAT) It's already happening...

MAN 1 Alright then.

MAN 2 We're doing it right after the wedding...

MAN 1 Okay.

MAN 2 In two days.

MAN 1 Alright.

MAN 2 Can you stand it that long...? Letting him kiss you like that...the way he does...and touch you the way he does...down there...?

MAN 1 He's...

MAN 2 What?

MAN 1 He likes it more when I do it...to him...touch him down there...

MAN 2 'Touch?'

MAN 1 Yeah. (BEAT) Well...with my tongue. And stuff. (BEAT) My mouth.

MAN 2 Okay. (BEAT) Okay. (BEAT) I'm gonna remember that...now you said it, I am really gonna remember that...

MAN 1 How do you mean?

MAN 2 When I'm doing it to him...what I'm gonna do...I'll keep that in mind.

That he likes having you do that to him...when I'm knocking his fucking teeth out, out on the pavement there...I'm gonna remember that...what he likes having you do.

MAN 1 Okay.

MAN 2 Yeah. Okay then.

MAN 2 GOES SILENT FOR A MOMENT AS HE TAKES ANOTHER BITE OF THE DANISH. PUTS IT DOWN. MAN 1 CHECKS HIS WATCH. GLANCES OVER AT MAN 2.

MAN 1 I should get going...

MAN 2 Yeah. You should.

MAN 1 I'm supposed to be out running...

MAN 2 I hear ya.

MAN 1 So...

MAN 2 Leave your hotel key there. On the table. (BEAT) For this room.

MAN 1 Okay.

MAN 2 Make sure it's the right one...this hotel key. Not the other one.

MAN 1 Fine.

MAN 1 CHECKS THEM BOTH CAREFULLY. PICKS UP ONE AND PUTS IT IN HIS POCKET.

MAN 2 And I'll see you soon...

MAN 1 Not that soon.

MAN 2 No. But soon. After the wedding.

MAN 1 Yep. (BEAT) But way after that...I mean...probably...

MAN 2 Uh-huh. However long it takes.

MAN 1 Right.

MAN 2 You shouldn't come back here again. (BEAT) 'Kay?

MAN 1 You're right.

MAN 2 I know I am.

MAN 1 Okay. (BEAT) See you.

MAN 2 Yeah. See you after.

MAN 1 Yes. After the wedding.

MAN 2 Exactly. When we live happily ever after...

MAN 1 You think so?

MAN 2 Yep.

MAN 1 Yeah?

MAN 2 Yes.

MAN 1 I hope so.

MAN 2 I know so. (BEAT) I know we will. (BEAT) Forever and ever and always.

MAN 2 GOES TO MAN 1. KISSES HIM ON THE CHEEK. HE TOUCHES HIS ARM AND SMILES AT HIM.

MAN 1 That's nice. I like that.

MAN 1 MOVES TO THE DOOR. LINGERS THERE. LOOKS AT MAN 2 ONE MORE TIME. FINALLY, HE GOES OUT. MAN 2 GETS UP, CROSSES TO THE FOOD LEFT BEHIND. PICKS UP A CHEESE DANISH. TOUCHES THE CHEESE WITH HIS FINGER. SNIFFS AT IT. LICKS IT. FINALLY SETS IT BACK DOWN. MAN 2 RETURNS TO HIS CHAIR. NEAR THE TV. STARING AT IT. MAN 2 SLOWLY CRACKS THE KNUCKLES ON EACH HAND. ONE BY ONE. SUDDENLY HE SITS UP, REMEMBERING.

MAN 2 (to himself) ...Sean Penn...

HE CONTINUES TO WATCH THE TV. SILENT. FLEXING HIS HANDS AND MAKING FISTS. AGAIN AND AGAIN.

THE FOURTH REICH

THE FOURTH REICH had its U.S. premiere at the Gaslight Theater as part of the 'LaBute New Theater Festival' in St. Louis Missouri in July 2018 and subsequently at the Davenport theater in New York as part of the 'NYC LaBute New Theater Festival' in January 2019. Both were directed by John Pierson.

Man – Eric Dean White

Eric Dean White
Photo: Patrick Huber

A MAN SITTING ON A CHAIR/BENCH ON STAGE. SMALL TABLE BESIDE HIM WITH A CARAFE OF WATER, A GLASS, A SMALL PAINTING IN A FRAME AND A BUD VASE WITH A FLOWER IN IT. MAN SMILES OUT AT US. WAITS. FINALLY SPEAKS:

BEGINNING #1 - (IF ACTOR IS WILLING TO FIELD POSSIBLE QUESTIONS FROM AUDIENCE)

...let's be clear about one thing and I think we can agree on that and start from there: Hitler lost. That's fair. He lost the war and, because of that, he has become one of the most maligned people in the history of the world...

WAITS.   Am I wrong about that or not? If I am, please, speak up...let me hear your thoughts and we'll go on after that.

WAITS.   Anyone? I mean it...seriously...can you think of too many other people who have suffered more bad shit written about them than this guy? And I'm saying warranted or not...either way, is there anybody else out there with more bad press about 'em than Adolf Hitler?

WAITS.   No. I thought so. Anyway, I think I'm being pretty reasonable when I say what I said before: "Hitler lost." Without question...he lost the war and so here we are today...dealing with that, all the...shit...that people say about him because of that.

BEGINNING #2 - (IF ACTOR ISN'T WILLING TO FIELD POSSIBLE QUESTIONS FROM AUDIENCE)

...let's be clear about one thing and I think we can agree on that and start from there: Hitler lost. That's fair. He lost the war and, because of that he has become one of the most maligned people in the history of the world...

I think I'm right about that.

I mean it...seriously...you can't think of too many other people who have suffered more bad shit written about them than this guy. And I'm saying warranted or not...either way, there really is nobody else out there with more bad press about 'em than Adolf Hitler.

And anyway, I think I'm being pretty reasonable when I say what I said before: "Hitler lost." Without question...he lost the war and so here we are today... dealing with that, all the...shit...that people say about him because of that. And, I mean, that's cool...you win and you get to do that...say whatever the hell you feel, but once the smoke's...you know...cleared or whatever...let's be honest: the man made some mistakes, that's what he did. Made a few mistakes. I mean... come on! Russia? What the fuck was that all about? Huh? Whoever in their right mind would secure a peace treaty with the Russians and then not stick to it? Who? I mean, at least until you've done everything that you wanna do going in the other direction...and he was close! He was SO close...what I mean is, if Germany could've put all their forces to work at one time against England—Battle of Britain or whatever they called it—can you imagine what would've happened? I mean, please, come on!

WAITS. But, like I said...to the victor goes the...you know...obviously the spoils, of course that, but a lot more than that, too. Way way more. *History.* You get to write history when you win...and that's what's happened in the case of Hitler... no question in my mind. The Allies won and so then they get to go and write all this nasty...petty...shit about Germany and the Nazis and...you know what I'm saying. Over and over and over with this Holocaust stuff and all the...just... whatever...anything they wanna say, they can just say it because, yes, Hitler lost...so guys in America and England and even in France...and, I mean, that kills me, the French saying shit about the war...that's unreal! WE FELL TO OUR KNEES LIKE A BUNCH OF PATHETIC BITCHES AND ROLLED OVER AND PLAYED DEAD FOR FIVE YEARS. That should be the name of any book a person from France ever writes on the subject of the Second World War. That...or, like...MY FAMILY TURNED IN OUR NEIGHBORS AND FRIENDS ON A REGULAR BASIS TO THE GESTAPO BECAUSE WE WERE SCARED AND AFRAID TO STAND UP FOR WHAT WE BELIEVED IN. And I know, I know, that couldn't actually be a title for a book that you'd sell in a store...but that's what all their books should be called... because that's who they were. Yes, there was the occasional resistance guy or even a lady who fought back...bombed stuff or smuggled weapons into the country and that kind of thing, but mostly, the French just went about their business...eating bread and making cheese and they simply added fucking Germans and helping them win the war to their list of daily chores. So...

WAITS. Obviously I have a few thoughts on the subject! Ha! And trust me, I'm French and my grandfather fought during the war, tail end of it—in the Pacific—and this is the way he felt about it, too. He felt the absolute same way as me and I have read lots and lots of writings by people, historians or whatever, who say basically the same thing as me…just in a less honest and straightforward way. I'm not saying the man was right in every thought, deed and action, no, I'm not saying that…what I am saying is this—these are the facts: he lifted his country upon high and then he lost the war. The rest…is conjecture. Subjective. Opinion.

WAITS. And the fucking French should have, like…little or nothing to say on the subject of World War Two. That is the truth. BUT they were part of the Allied Forces and the war is over and we win…"WE"—thanks to the Russians, pretty much, and not taking anything away from the US and England, who fought hard in a number of really tough and ugly campaigns in Africa and Italy and Europe… but those tough-as-nails Russians…! Those guys just do not give up…they do not know the meaning of it. For centuries, pounded on every side by some invading force, year after year after year…and they just keep coming back. You look at pictures from those battles over there—Moscow and…and…Stalingrad…places like that…it is just insane. In-sane. It's freezing cold, no food, no guns, like… nothing…they had literally not one thing to push back this man and his war machine…and yet…somehow…they do it. I mean, it took, like, 20 million people or some crazy…or is that how many people Stalin killed? I dunno, I get some of that stuff mixed up, but whatever it was, they hold on. Not like Britain did, all that…'be calm and carry on' bullshit, the Russians fought hand-to-hand, right back across a few thousand miles of the deadliest tracts of land know to man… right back to the streets of Berlin until the job is done…I mean…unheard of. Unprecedented. Impossible, almost…but they did it.

WAITS. And…listen… I'm not even particularly fond of the Russians, overall, I'm really not, but you've gotta look at what they did there and kind of marvel at it…it was pretty extraordinary. The…just…sheer…*will* to survive as a people and as a country.

WAITS. So…yeah…the French should just shut up about the war…or at least not say shit about Hitler and whatever he accomplished because, yes…as I have already conceded, he lost, he did, fine...but he actually had a few very smart things to say about life and politics and...warfare—the Jews, of course—all of those subjects...but it's just "baby with the bathwater" every time in these sort of situations and it shouldn't be! It just really...shouldn't...the man is dead... he paid for his sins...but he had some interesting things to say, along the way... he really did. That's all I'm saying. Truth is...if you read his work...actually take the time to sit down and read what he thought, what he—at great cost to him- self—took the time to put down on paper...books like MEIN KAMPF and those things—the man was not stupid. He wasn't stupid...he wasn't crazy...

WAITS. He LOST.

WAITS. Now, that might not be the most popular idea to put forth, that it was not the man himself who messed up so much as the people who promised him the world...to go to the ends of the earth and to die for him...but not all of them were telling the truth, now, were they? No, uh-uh, they were not...turns out a few of them liked wearing the uniform around, they liked that part—and those were things of just absolute beauty, I will give you that, stand up and take a bow, Mr. Hugo Boss! GREAT-looking uniforms—and it was all fun and games when Po- land fell and Czechoslovakia and France and blah-blah-blah...it was a blast to be a German and a Nazi and all that when things were rolling along but as soon as things started to go sideways...England and then Africa, couple of battles to the East...in Italy...that is when the whispers begin. "He's a madman...he's unstable... he'll get us all killed..." People are just such...fucking...fair-weather friends, aren't they? I mean, for the most part...jump ship the second—and I mean the very first fucking second—that things go wrong. That was Germany. Loved it during the 30s...when it was all smiles and U-Boats and the economy is recover- ing nicely, thank you very much...but as things start going back the other way... the mice just...spill off the fucking ship. Ain't that just always the way? Always.

WAITS. Listen, I'm an American and none of this is even my business, I mean... not really...but I just hate it any time I see somebody getting ganged up on...beat up by a bunch of folks who say this and that...don't even check the fucking facts and get all whatever about things...history...without knowing the story behind the story, because there always is one. Isn't there? Yes, there is...and there was here too. There was. Six million Jews. That's all anybody ever talks about in relation to Hitler and everything else he did...six million Jews. Ok, ok! Yes, that's a LOT of people! I give you that...but that's it? That's where the conversation stops? Not for me it doesn't, and for me—living in America and free to think clear and rational thougths, it just doesn't have to end there either—my God, people see a picture of a pile of bodies and they go nuts...absolutely nuts. Pile of bodies, pile of bodies...like it's the worst thing that *ever* happened in the history of the world. Well, lemme tell you this...it's not. There are worse things than a pile of bodies. Like: no bodies. None. Bodies that were obliterated. How about that? You wanna see pictures, take a look at a few from a little place called Nagasaki. Or how about Hiroshima? No bodies there...because we blew 'em to smithereens. WE did that...US. So just—listen, a man is never just one thing. That is definitely bad. The Jew thing, definitely goes in the "cons" column, if we're doing that, pros and cons—BUT that is not the beginning and the end of who Hitler was and all the legacy he left behind. It's just not, otherwise you have to trash all of 'em, every last one of these guys who had to kill some people to create what they did: Mao and, and Stalin and Pol Pot and Grant and... yeah...let's not leave him out...Ulysses S. Grant...just because we don't wanna equate the American Indian in the same breath as the six million—the sacred six million—but anybody who can think clearly and rationally and realistically are gonna say..."yes, that was a clear and obvious case of extreme mass genocide..." The Americas. South and North. The numbers are just...so high and so shocking—read Dobyns sometime and I promise you, your mouth will fall to the fucking floor at some of his estimates—but those numbers whither if asked to stand next to the precious...the glorious...the untouchable six million. But why? WHY?!

WAITS. Don't ask me...

WAITS. And what about me? Hmmmm? Should I be tossed out in the garbage 'cause of one bad thing I did, years ago, when I was a kid? These days I work with people, in the community, I'm a coach to children on the weekends... lead church activities...should all of that mean nothing because of a rock I threw one time? One stone thrown in anger at some other child...does that negate a lifetime? I don't think so. And I know, I know...that isn't the same thing as what I was talking about before...the men who have destroyed entire...I'm not saying that it is, I'm just pointing out that a person is never just one thing. A single thought. A single Gesture. Action. We're too complex for that...and it would be good to take all that into consideration when judging the man. Anyhow, that's what I did...and I came out the other side with a deep and abiding respect for a man who dreamed large, who reached high...who took an entire nation onto his back and carried them up the side of a mountain...nearly to the top. Almost to the very pinnacle of it, only to become a punch-line some seventy years later. That is a very deep and sobering message to me...and it should be to any and all of you, too, sitting out there and listening to me tonight. Not about him... but about people. People in general.

All of this I say to you without turning over cars or fighting in the street or any of that...I say it in normal tones using my "inside voice" and appealing to your intellect and to your sense of right and wrong and human compassion...I say all this to you because I believe it to be true...and honest...and fair. He was a man. He made mistakes. Ok. Was he a monster? Was he evil? I'm not sure I even know what that word means...anymore. If evil does exist, it is in the very way that we call other things by that name. Without any proof...without any facts... simply because we can. So we do. But why? Why do we?...because it makes us feel better about ourselves? I dunno...but we do it and with it we create fear... and you know where that can lead. Oh, yes you do...

Give the man a chance, that's all I'm asking here. Read his book...study every-thing that happened in those days...not just the official accounts but everything. A picture will start to form...the portrait of a man who said "yes I can" and "yes I will" at a time when no one else had the courage or the guts or the balls to do the same...!

WAITS. "Adolf Hitler."

WAITS. Even the name is outlawed these days...obviously his last name, "Hitler," obviously that...but even his first name! His given name. Adolf. You never hear anyone being christened that anymore. Never. And why? Why? Because of that one guy? REALLY? It's just...God, it's crazy. The world is sometimes just– I can't even begin to explain it, and that makes me sad, it really does...how easily we forget. How quickly we turn away from something or someone. When we decide it's no longer for us...that it'd be easier or better or smarter to go the other way, to join the other side. It's just...I guess I'll just leave it at that. How quickly and easily we as human beings are capable of doing that...saying ME TOO and joining the ranks of the mob. It frightens me, I'm not kidding you.

WAITS.   We point our fingers and gnash our teeth and bring others down... then we turn out backs and forget them, and pretend that they never existed... and if that's not a sin—how easily we do that, turn on each other—then I don't know what one is.

WAITS.   There. That wasn't so bad, was it? I didn't scream or threaten or spew hatred at you...did I? I just sat here, in my little chair with my little table, and my little bud vase and my...little painting... (POINTS TO THE PAINTING). Do you like it? The painting? It's probably hard to see from there...but it's a little landscape. Quite pretty. Now it's not a Turner or Monet or Constable but I like it. Very hard to come by. Took me many years to track it down and pay for it but I have it now... it's mine and I hang it very proudly in my home—in a place of honor-- I'm sure you can guess the artist. Can't you? Yes. Of course you can...

WAITS.   I own it because I love it and that is all that matters. Nothing else. I don't have to justify it and you don't have to like it but I have no problem—at all—dividing it from the legacy of the man who made it...even though, as you've heard, I don't have much of a problem with his legacy, either. And why?

WAITS.   Because I don't live in a world of fear...I don't wallow in an empire of hearsay. I listen and I read and I remain open...open to the truth, no matter how hard or tough or...ugly...it may be. I believe in what is true and right and reasonable.

WAITS.   Don't be afraid. The truth will set you free. Look at it. Really look. There is nothing there to fear. A building. Some trees and mountains. Sky. Some watercolor paint and a piece of paper.

WAITS.   This is "art," no matter whom the artist is. It is a thing of beauty and something to be savored...not savaged. Look at it. Really look.

WAITS.   The composition. The color. Formal and serene. There is nothing to be afraid of here...nothing to hate. Look at it again. Really look this time...

WAITS. It's just a picture...of a world...all fresh and new...waiting...waiting for something great to begin.

WAITS. A world painted by a young artist, one who had to live with his own fears...a terrible father...lean and hungry years...rejection from an institution that he longed to be a part of—twice!—a horrible ghastly war. All those things. BUT when he painted...when he was able to step outside himself and be free... free to paint things as he saw them...then, for just a moment, for a single fleeting second...he was filled with hope, hope and dreams and desire. Desire for a new and better day...for you and me.

WAITS. That's what I see...when I look at it...don't you? No? Are you sure?

WAITS. Look again. Once more. Really look.

WAITS. Can you feel it? It's there. The future...our future...*ours*. The living. The upcoming future that is ours to dictate and decide: to live as we want and then write the history of. That's what I see in those colors there. A golden promise of tomorrow and forever. It's there...I swear it is. You only have to reach out and touch it...that's all.

WAITS. Don't be afraid. Just lean forward in your chairs there and take one more look...you'll see what I mean.

WAITS. It's right there.

WAITS. I know you can do it...I know you can.

WAITS. See it. Touch it. Believe it.

WAITS. You have nothing to fear...I promise you.

WAITS Ab-so-lute-ly nothing at all...

THE MAN HOLDS THE PAINTING TOWARD US. SMILING. IMPLORING.

GREAT NEGRO WORKS OF ART

GREAT NEGRO WORKS OF ART had its world premiere at the Davenport theater in New York as part of the 'NYC LaBute New Theater Festival' in January 2019 and subsequently at the Gaslight Theater as part of the 'LaBute New Theater Festival' in St. Louis Missouri in July 2019. Both were directed by John Pierson.

Tom: KeiLyn Durrel Jones (Jaz Tucker – STL)
Jerri: Brenda Meaney (Carly Rosenbaum – STL)

A slash (/) indicates where the next actor should speak.

(left to right) Brenda Meaney, KeiLyn Durrel Jones
Photo: Russ Rowland

LIGHTS UP TO REVEAL A SIDE GALLERY IN A MUSEUM. A FEW BENCHES ON THE FLOOR AND ART WORK ON THE WALLS. A WOMAN STANDING BY HERSELF. STARING UP AT A PAINTING. LET'S CALL HER JERRI. 20S, SWEET, ATTRACTIVE, A BIT NERVOUS. WHITE. SHE'S CARRYING A PAMPHLET IN ONE HAND. SHE CHECKS HER WATCH, WAITS A BIT, THEN BACK TO THE PAINTING. AFTER A MOMENT A MAN ENTERS, SEES HER, AND CROSSES TO HER. HE IS CARRYING FLOWERS. HANDS THEM TO HER WHEN IT'S TIME. THIS IS TOM. ABOUT THE SAME AGE, WELL-DRESSED, HANDSOME BUT DOESN'T QUITE BELIEVE IT. BLACK. A TINY LITTLE HUG. TENTATIVE, QUICK.

TOM   ...hey there, I'm so sorry that I'm late! Really, it was...anyway, I'm sorry. (BEAT) I'm Tom, in case you are not Jerri...who I'm supposed to be meeting. Here. At the museum.

JERRI   I am, that's me. Jerri. Hi.

TOM   Hello!

JERRI   Yeah. Hi. Hello. (ABOUT FLOWERS) And thanks for these...so sweet.

MOMENT OF PAUSE. THAT LONG BEAT BEFORE TWO PEOPLE JUMP INTO SOMETHING THEY'RE BOTH UNSURE ABOUT. HE SMILES AND THEN:

JERRI   ...so.

TOM   It's funny, right?

JERRI   What's that?

TOM   Us...being named that. 'Tom and Jerri.'

JERRI   Is it?

TOM   Just...yeah, a little. I mean, us meeting up like this and our names being what they are...like the famous cartoon. (BEAT) When I realized the connection, it made me laugh...

JERRI   Oh. Right. 'Tom and Jerry.' (BEAT) I didn't even think of that...

TOM   No?

JERRI   Until you just said it, no--mine is spelled differently, so--but you're right, it's kind of funny.

TOM   Yeah. Not like 'funny funny' but, you know...'funny odd.' That's all. Ironic.

JERRI   Yep...

A LULL IN THE CHAT AND TOM IS QUICK TO TRY AND FILL THE VOID.

TOM   Again, sorry, I got stuck on a call at work--have you done this thing yet, they have online, it's called 'Google Hang-Out?' It's just...it's not like hanging out at all...they made it for conferences, you know, like conference calls...but they wanna make it sound cool and hip and all that so, yeah...they give it a name like that. 'Google Hang-Out.' (BEAT) It's dumb but that's what I was doing. Hanging out...with a bunch of people from L.A. whom I've never met before...so that was fun. (BEAT) Anyway, I'm sorry but here I am. Late but...still interested...so yeah. (BEAT) Hi. (BEAT) I'm Tom.

JERRI   Hi, Tom.

TOM   Hi.

JERRI   It's no problem, honestly. You getting here now...

TOM   Great...yeah...I just grabbed some flowers and dashed over...

JERRI   Today's my day off so it's fine for me...doesn't matter that you were late, it's all good. I was just taking in the exhibit... (BEAT) What does that mean? 'Still interested?'

TOM   Oh, no, sorry! That's just a joke.

JERRI   I don't get it.

TOM   Just...you know! You set a thing like this up...on some app...and you just... you never know until you get there what's waiting for you...on the other side.

JERRI   And so...what's the joke part...?

TOM   Like...who you're gonna get!

JERRI   Oh...

TOM   Ha! No, I just mean--I think you're great, you are, and you look a lot like your profile picture, which is rare--but I just mean sometimes. Sometimes it's way different when you finally meet up with a person. That's all. (BEAT) Talking is not one of my strengths, by the way...I tend to babble...so please stop me before I embarrass myself!

JERRI   No, that's really kind. Thanks.

TOM   For...what...?

JERRI   For calling me great.

TOM   Oh...well...I mean it. I like the way you look and everything. I do.

JERRI   That's nice. (BEAT) And that's why you're still interested?

TOM   No, come on...that's just a term...that's a thing that people say, all the time...and I am. I like what I see--meaning you--so yes, I'm still interested.

JERRI   Ok.

TOM   Is it?

JERRI   Yes. Absolutely ok.

TOM   Good.

JERRI   So, then...let's...ha! I don't know what to say now. I'm a little flustered by all this!

TOM   Sorry! (BEAT) I'm not lying...

JERRI   I didn't think you were.

TOM   Alright, good.

JERRI   Do you lie a lot or something...? I mean generally...in life?

TOM   No...not that much. About like most people, I guess.

JERRI   Oh. (BEAT) Is there an average?

TOM   I don't know! See? I'm babbling...!

JERRI   That's ok, I'm the one who asked...

TOM True, but...

JERRI So you're not a 'liar?'

TOM No, not at all!

JERRI You just...you lie sometimes...

TOM Yeah. Like everybody.

JERRI I don't lie.

TOM Oh.

JERRI I mean, I try not to. It's a thing with me...my dad was a liar. He was a terrible liar and ruined my life, a lot of it, anyway, when I was a kid--divorce and different schools and all kinds of things, summers in places that I didn't wanna be--so I pretty much hate liars. Loathe 'em, actually. Even the word I hate.

TOM Wow...ok...yeah...understood.

JERRI So, you're not one? Right?

TOM No...not like that! Not like 'end a family and ruin everything' kind of person. Not on that scale. At all. Just little...white..../ Anyway!

JERRI Well, good. That's good./ Yeah, anyway! I'm glad that you made it. I was starting to wonder a little, but...you stopped for *flowers*...

TOM I know! Forgive me!

JERRI No, I'm kidding...no worries...I'd heard good things about the exhibit anyway, so even if you hadn't made it, I would've been happy to come.

TOM Cool.

JERRI Uh-huh.

TOM "GREAT NEGRO WORKS OF ART."

JERRI Yeah...

TOM Is that something you're into?

JERRI What's that?

TOM Negroes?

JERRI …

TOM I'm joking! That's just a little joke…obviously. (BEAT) Kidding.

JERRI …ok…and yes, I like black men.

TOM Good! Good for me…

JERRI Oh, you're black? I had no idea…I thought you were Mexican.

TOM SMILES AT THIS--HE LIKES THE HUMOR--SO HE THROWS THE JOKE BACK AT HER, THIS TIME EVEN HARDER:

TOM I am, but don't tell anyone…I don't wanna give up my welfare check.

SHE LOOKS AT HIM STRANGELY, NOT SURE HOW TO REACT--HE KNOWS HE'S PROBABLY GONE TOO FAR SO HE SMILES AND SAYS:

TOM JOKE! (BEAT) And I shouldn't play around with something like that… people are so sensitive these days, about everything, every little word we say. All that 'cancel' shit. (BEAT) But not me--I'm not.

JERRI No?

TOM Uh-uh. It's gotten ridiculous…every phrase is so loaded, it's become perilous, jut trying to have a conversation today…and not just men and women… everybody. (BEAT) I can't stand it.

JERRI I know what you mean.

TOM Yeah?

JERRI Sure. (BEAT) I mean, it's important to say what you mean and to realize that there are some things that are probably off-limits, or at least off-limits to various groups of peple…but…yes, I'd agree with you. Overall, I mean.

TOM Thanks.

JERRI Welcome.

THEY SMILE AT EACH OTHER, THEN TURN TO LOOK AT THE PAINTING IN FRONT OF THEM.

TOM Art.

JERRI Yep.

TOM Are you an 'art lover?'

JERRI I kind of am. Yes.

TOM Yeah, I think it said that in your thingie if I'm not mistaken…

JERRI My…what…?

TOM Your…you know…'likes & dislikes.' (BEAT) In your profile.

JERRI Oh, right! That! Yes! It does say that I'm…that I enjoy art.

TOM I remember…

JERRI Of course. That's why we're here.

TOM Because of 'art?'

JERRI No, not just that…but because we connected on a number of details… art being one of them.

TOM Right. (BEAT) I like Art.

JERRI Me too. And Dance..the Outdoors…both recent graduates.

TOM Yep. That's…you are…and me too and so we're here. That's awesome.

JERRI I agree. I'm glad.

TOM So…did you…have you looked at the whole thing yet or did you save some of it for me?

JERRI Oh no, I waited…I checked out the little things over there…what're those called…the… (LOOKING IN HER PAMPHLET) 'Lawn jockeys' but that's about it…

TOM That's great. What'd you think?

JERRI About…?

TOM   The statues...

JERRI   Oh, they're...you know...cute.

TOM   'Cute?'

JERRI   No, not 'cute' but...you know...interesting.

TOM   'Interesting.'

JERRI   Just...yeah. They're historic. Right? Aren't they? I think so. It said they were, on the little label thingie...these are reproductions made from melted down rap albums to commemorate the past.

TOM   Huh. That's cool. (BEAT) They were hitching posts...during the slave trade. That's what they were for, to welcome other white folks onto the plantation... and people have just perpetuated that by keeping 'em around. (BEAT) But that's what they are...if that's what you mean by *historic*.

JERRI   Oh.

TOM   I guess some people paint 'em different colors and consider 'em art, now, too...I mean, whoever added these to the exhibit, anyway.

JERRI   I guess so...

TOM   I wonder if it's a black artist who made those or a white one?

JERRI   Hmmmm...I don't know...

TOM   Doesn't say anything there in your pamphlet?

JERRI   I don't think so...I didn't notice if it did. (READING) No...although I think the whole exhibit's dedicated to...you know...

TOM   What?

JERRI   You know.

TOM   No, what?

JERRI   Black artists. Of color.

TOM Oh.

JERRI I think that's why it's called... (READING) But lemme look again.

TOM That's not really a term, just so you know. 'Black artists of color.'

JERRI Oh. Of course not...I just...

TOM It's usually just one or the other.

JERRI Right.

TOM Just to be clear.

JERRI Absolutely. (BEAT) Does it matter, though...? Which one it is...? Is there one you prefer today...?

TOM I mean...

JERRI Your community? I'm just asking...I'm not an authority, obviously.

TOM But I am?

JERRI No! That's not...I just mean...you would probably know more than me... being from...you know...

TOM Where? (BEAT) Africa?

JERRI No, please...! (BEAT) You're not really from Africa...are you...?

TOM I mean...originally.

JERRI Come on...

TOM I'm serious. My great-greats.

JERRI Ok, well, no. I didn't mean that...I wasn't implying anything about...

TOM I'm kidding with you...

JERRI ...ok...

TOM I am, but it's true...some people think that's art...they don't just put 'em on their lawns for fun...and you know what...? People don't know shit about 'em, not really...I don't mean to swear, but...they just think it's cool to have some little black sambo statue in the front yard wearing his riding silks or some velvety suit! (BEAT) Did you know that there are actually two kinds of lawn jockeys, Jerri? Did you?

JERRI I think...maybe I've heard that...

TOM No, come on, be honest! You did not know that...

JERRI Alright, no, that's...I might not know the exact history...of those things... but...I'm...

SHE STRUGGLES TO FIND SOMETHING TO SAY SO HE JUMPS IN AGAIN:

TOM They both have names. One's *jocko* which is usually the shorter kind, the hunched over little black-faced boy, with his toothy grin and big eyes and shit... and the other is a taller, more dignified version, wearing a suit and that one, he's called *cavalier spirit*. (BEAT) You ever read Flannery O'Conner? That story, THE ARTIFICIAL NIGGER?/ You should.

JERRI Ahhh, no, but I will.../ He's an author I like, so I'll do that...

SILENCE AS TOM LOOKS AT HER FOR A LONG BEAT, THEN STATES:

TOM Flannery O'Connor is a woman.

JERRI Oh, ok...I thought it was a man.

TOM I thought you liked his work...

JERRI I thought I did, too, but I must be thinking of the wrong person ...some other writer named 'O'Connor.'

TOM I guess so.

JERRI Sorry.

TOM No, it's not a problem, I'm not trying to make you feel bad...

JERRI Well, I kind of do now...

TOM Sorry, that's not what I was trying to do...I just wanted you to see...

JERRI   Anyway...I like James Baldwin.

TOM   Oh.

JERRI   I read NATIVE SON in school and I thought it was really moving...and I saw the movie of it, too. There might be more than one but I saw the one that Oprah was in. That version.

TOM   Okay...

JERRI   And Toni Morrison...I like her, too. I didn't read that book...THE COLOR PURPLE, but I thought the film was fantastic. And BELOVED as well--those were both good. (BEAT) And those had Oprah acting in them, too...I never thought about that until now, but they all did... (BEAT) She's an excellent actor.

TOM   Yeah. She's good.

JERRI   You don't think so...?

TOM   No, I do. I like her.

JERRI   I feel like you're just saying that to make me feel better now...

TOM   Why would I be trying to make *you* feel better...?

JERRI   No, not because you HAVE TO, but because you WANT TO, because you're nice and because we had the weird little thing there...about those hitching posts and the author you recommended that I didn't know...so now you're...I dunno...trying to say what I wanna hear, because you're a gentleman or whatever... (BEAT) Is that what you're doing or am I totally reading this wrong...? I might be but I didn't think so...

TOM HESITATES A MOMENT BUT THEN NODS AND SMILES AT HER AS HE SAYS:

TOM   Yeah, no, you're right...that's what I was doing. Trying to make things nice again.

JERRI   Well, that's...I appreciate that. It's very sweet. A lot of people wouldn't give a shit--see? I can swear, too--they'd get angry for no reason, or, not 'no' reason but for hardly any reason...a mistake I made about knowing some fact and that would be it...they'd start making excuses about work or not feeling well or whatever and they'd try to get out of our evening together, because of that one thing…even if they did find me attractive, which you seem to do, but even then… because I offended them by saying one wrong word or not knowing something or knowing too much about another thing or…you know what I'm saying, right? Has this happened to you? I'm guessing it has, if you're out there meeting people online but maybe not…maybe it's just me. It could be, but I doubt it… (BEAT) Is it? Is it just me or have you noticed the same thing? Be honest.

TOM   No…that's very…yes. I have. I absolutely have. People are just WAY too sensitive today. About…you know…everything. Feminist stuff and race stuff and, and…all of it. I totally agree with you about what it's like out there now…people pointing a finger at each other over any little thing! It's crazy…it's not a way to live and so, no, I'm glad that you're not that way…I'm glad you're just 'you.'

JERRI   Well, great. Thanks.

TOM   Thank YOU.

JERRI   I'm glad that we're…you know…that we're still ok here. That's good.

TOM   I'm glad, too…

THEY SHARE A QUICK LITTLE HUG. NOTHING SEXUAL, JUST FRIENDLY.

JERRI   I like you. I mean, the way you look and your personality and all that stuff. I can be finicky about guys, but I'm impressed so far…

TOM   Ha! Thanks! That's nice…saying it out loud like that…

JERRI   Well, usually I'm a little shy and I think I lose out on things, because of it, so I thought why not? Just say what you mean, what harm can there be in that? (BEAT) Right?

TOM   None at all…far as I'm concerned.

JERRI   I agree! The truth sets you free…

TOM   Absolutely!

JERRI   Wonderful!

TOM   Great! Then let's do this...let's have a date!

JERRI   Yes, please! I'm ready!

TOM   I know you are...you were on time.

JERRI   Early, actually...

TOM   Oh, I'm sorry...

JERRI   Oh, let's not go there again! No more 'sorry' between us...let's move on! Move forward!

TOM   Ok, cool, can do...sorry! (BEAT) AHHH! Sorry! I won't say it again! I'm through saying sorry. Promise! (BEAT) Anyway...

THEY HAVE ANOTHER QUIET MOMENT, LOOKING FOR THE NEXT SUBJECT OR THE NEXT ANYTHING TO KEEP THIS LITTLE MEETING AFLOAT.

JERRI   "GREAT NEGRO WORKS OF ART."

TOM   Yep.

JERRI   It's provocative.

TOM   Is it?

JERRI   Kind of...calling a museum show by that name. I think so...

TOM   Yeah, maybe it is...

JERRI   Feels like it. Today, especially...with things the way they are.

TOM   No, yeah--I get what you're saying.

JERRI   It's...is that correct, or should it be..."GREAT WORKS OF NEGRO ART"? (BEAT) I don't even feel comfortable using that word any more as a woman... without color...because it goes in and out of fashion so much, but you can...I'm sure you can get away with it, so which is it? NEGRO or ARTS first? You tell me...

TOM   ...

JERRI   I'm just asking. Do you think they mean that the art is great, or...?

TOM   It's...I dunno, I'm...would it be better? The other way around...?

JERRI   It's just...you know...it'd keep those two words together at the top, "GREAT WORKS" and that makes more sense to me...or just "GREAT NEGRO ART," even, but you're the--

TOM   What? (BEAT) The what? Authority?

JERRI   No! Please, let's not do that one again...I'm sorry about before...

TOM   And I'm kidding! I don't know any better than you...they could mean the art's great or the people who made it are great...we never even found out if it's all black artists or not...so...

JERRI   Yeah, I looked in the pamphlet but it doesn't really say...

TOM   ...hmmmm...

JERRI   There's no pictures, so...not sure.

TOM   So let's just enjoy it...or not...

JERRI   Meaning....?

TOM   Meaning let's just feel about it however we end up feeling about it. Without preconceived notions...

JERRI   Sounds great... (BEAT) I really do prefer "GREAT NEGRO ART." That's the easiest to remember...

TOM   Yeah. That's good...concise.

THEY MOVE TO THE NEXT PAINTING. STUDYING IT. AFTER A BEAT:

TOM   I bet you don't know too many black artists, though, do you? I mean, in reality...

JERRI   Ummmmmmmmmm...

TOM   Just off hand. Just off the top of your head...do you, Jerri?

JERRI   You mean...like...?

TOM Like Picasso. Like Pollack.

JERRI Picasso wasn't black...was he?

TOM Ha! You tell me...

JERRI No, I don't mean he was 'black' black...like...you know...

TOM Like me.

JERRI Is that ok to say?

TOM You can say whatever you wanna say. Go ahead.

JERRI No, I just mean...you're...what...?

TOM I dunno...what would you call me?

JERRI Oh God...why do I let myself get into this...look, I'm just saying that you're pretty black, like a much darker black...that's all...

TOM ...ok...

JERRI Is that true or not?

TOM You are correct...but...not everybody makes that same distinction in this country...between different...

JERRI Well, I do...

TOM Which?

JERRI Just...between very black people and other ones, like, who are obviously more...of a 'mix'...with some other race in there as well...

TOM Ok. And the distinction is...?

JERRI Just that...there is a difference, I guess. That's all...

TOM And that means...?

JERRI Nothing! It's just genetics and interesting...how one person can be so black--super black--and then one can be light. With freckles.

TOM   Exactly! Same as you.

JERRI   Yep! (SMILES) I do have a few…

TOM   Yeah. It's…wild…right?

JERRI   And I'm not an art historian or anything like that, but I know Picasso was from Spain and all the pictures I've ever seen of him he looks very tan… very dark brown…and I think there was, you know…back in olden times, in Spain…wasn't there some kind of big…what-would-you-call-it? Influx of that kind of thing…blacks…into that country? And I'm not talking about today, the whole immigrant problem, not them, I mean way back when. That group.

TOM   The Moors…

JERRI   Yes. That's who I mean! Them.

TOM   Who?

JERRI   The Moors! The ones from back in the Crusades and all that, from Northern Africa, who rose up to fight the Christians…who came and fought with them.

TOM   I don't know if that's…

JERRI   What?

TOM   They didn't 'come' to fight the Crusaders…that's not…

JERRI   Ummmmmmmm…

TOM   The Crusaders came to them…into their homes and killed them and so, yes, they fought back but the real aggression came from the North…not the other way around.

JERRI   Oh. (BEAT) Maybe so.

TOM   No, not maybe so, it did…that's the way it happened. In history.

JERRI   Ok, fine, I'm not sure, so if you know it for a fact, then fine…

TOM   I do.

JERRI Is that the part of Africa you're from...I mean, originally?

TOM What?

JERRI That's what YOU said! That you were from there...or your people were... or whatever, so I'm asking if you meant from Morocco or Egypt or...just because you seem to know so much about it, so I just assumed.

TOM No, I know it because it happened that way and I've studied it...that's how I know.

JERRI You sound angry now.

TOM Not at all, no...I just think...

JERRI But the Moors did go up into Spain at some point, right? They did do that...I'm pretty sure...

TOM Yes, they did...AFTER they'd been attacked for many years...many many years...they were able to drive the Crusaders out of the Holy Land and then pushed them back into Spain...which then caused what I think you were alluding to...a darkening of the skin and all that...in Spain...for a period of time.

JERRI See? I knew that happened.

TOM Yeah, but after all the other...

JERRI But I don't think Picasso was black or anything...even with all of that happening. In Spain, I mean...

TOM No. You're right... (BEAT) Picasso was not black.

JERRI Ok, good.

TOM It's good that he wasn't black...?

JERRI No! I'm just glad that there wasn't a fact like that floating around out there and I didn't know it...that would've been embarrassing.

TOM I see.

JERRI Yeah. Anyway...

TOM   Yep. Anyway. (BEAT) All I was saying is that you probably don't know very many black artists...not like you do white artists. Like Picasso, or Pollack or people like that...Warhol and Rothko and Cassatt and Van Gogh and on and on and on...! (BEAT) Can you name any? Just a couple? Even one? (BEAT) Can you, Jerri?

SHE STANDS THERE, LOOKING AT HIM AND RACKING HER BRAIN FOR A NAME OR TWO. NOTHING POPS INTO HER HEAD.

JERRI   Didn't know I was coming here to get quizzed or I would've studied up... sorry.

TOM   No, don't be mad...that's not...

JERRI   Just thought this might be nice...to see this exhibit together, but if I thought it was gonna make you get all uppity about it, then I--

TOM   'Uppity!'

JERRI   You know what I'm saying! God!!

TOM   I know that we're both trying to be nice here..but that's not a word that I feel very comfortable with...

JERRI   Well, it doesn't feel very nice right now...not at all.

TOM   I'm sorry, I want it to be but I was just curious! Sorry, it just gets me going sometimes, when someone says they love something, but they don't really--

JERRI   What? (BEAT) What? Go ahead...

TOM   No, just that...it's...

JERRI   I do love art. I do and I always have so please don't tell me that I don't... because I would actually find that a little offensive...

TOM   But you don't know the names of any negro artists...not one...

JERRI   Not just off-hand, no! I'm not like some trivia champion, I'm sorry...!

TOM   No, come on, that's not what I'm...

JERRI   What?

TOM Basquiat? Do you know him?

JERRI It sounds familiar...

TOM Jerri, come on...!

JERRI WHAT?

TOM Nothing. No, forget it. (SMILES) It doesn't matter...honestly. It's ok. I just thought that maybe--

JERRI I mean...no, probably not...I don't know many black artists but they're not very famous, are they? I mean, not really...or I would...because that's who people know--and I mean regular people like me--we get to know someone's name when they become famous...super famous. Now, maybe it's because these guys are fine artists and so they think it's beneath them, like they don't have to go out there and try to be famous and that's fine but...it's not my fault I don't know them...it's not, and look, I know lots of black people in the arts. LOTS. The 'arts' meaning movies and music and, and...Beyonce. I know her...everybody knows her: because she's FAMOUS. Very very famous. Denzel Washington, he's so famous that we just call him 'Denzel.' Oprah, who I mentioned before: same thing. Famous. Miles Davis and Billie Holiday and who's that other one? The dance one? Alvin Ailey...and on and on and on...those are all artists that I know who're black and I love their work...just like the rest of the world. (BEAT) I can't help it about these other ones...like the person you mentioned...these other artists, they need to hurry up and get famous and then I'll know who they are. (BEAT) That's up to them.

TOM IS ABOUT TO SAY SOMETHING BUT HE STOPS HIMSELF. HE IS STILL TRYING TO LIKE THIS PERSON AND SO HE BOTTLES UP WHAT HE WAS ABOUT TO SAY.

TOM No, you're right...we do tend to learn about people that way...as people get famous.

JERRI It is true...and anyway...

TOM What?

JERRI Nothing.

TOM   No, go ahead...please...

JERRI   It's also because I'm white, so...of course I'm more likely to know a lot more white artists than black ones. Don't you think that's why? I do...I think that's completely logical and true...

TOM   Ummmmmmmm...maybe...but...

JERRI   You disagree...?

TOM   That's part of it, sure, but...

JERRI   It's race and gender, both... (BEAT) I could name a bunch of famous female country singers right now if I wanted to...can you?

TOM   I mean...a couple probably...

JERRI   'Probably.'

TOM   Yes. Probably.

JERRI   Then do it...go ahead.

TOM   ...

JERRI   Go on. Name one.

SHE STARTS HUMMING THE THEME SONG FROM "JEOPARDY!" AS TOM STRUGGLES FOR A MOMENT BUT CAN'T THINK OF ANYONE. HE SHRUGS, BUT THEN SUDDENLY FEELS INSPIRED.

TOM   Those girls...the three...you know! Come on...the, ummmm...they pissed off the president and they're...The Dixie Chicks! (SMILES) There! See?

JERRI   That's a group...three women who sing together...not *a* singer...and they're called 'The Chicks' now, they changed their name...

TOM   So? At least I got it right.

JERRI   Yeah? Then name one. Name 1 chick.

TOM   What?

JERRI   Any of the three. By <u>name</u>. (BEAT) Go ahead.

TOM   Of for God's sake! That's...

HE HAS NO IDEA WHAT THEIR NAMES ARE. HE THROWS HIS HANDS UP AND GIVES IN AS JERRI NODS AND SAYS:

JERRI   See? Not so easy, is it? Off the cuff, I mean. Now, is that because of the fact that they're women...or because they're white? You tell me.

TOM   I dunno! Because...they're...not...

JERRI   ...it's because black people don't like country. Or very few, anyway, so it makes sense. (BEAT) <u>See?</u> And that's why I don't know the names of many black artists...

TOM   WHAT? Any. You don't know any.

JERRI   Fine! Any.

TOM   But...

JERRI   And that's why, I'm sure of it.

TOM IS TRYING TO HOLD IT IN BUT HE FINALLY CAN'T, SO HE SAYS:

TOM   It could be...might also have something to do with exhibits like this one... hidden away in the back gallery of the back wing of some museum and given a name like this--which we do agree on...that it's confusing and meaningless and keeps perpetuating the idea that we're not good enough--us black people, both the really really black ones AND the other ones too--that we're not good enough to be hanging on the walls with everybody else...out where all the museumgoers can see 'em...that could be another reason that you don't know Basquiat or Kara Walker or Kehinde Wiley or any artist of color. None.

JERRI   Maybe. (BEAT) Yeah, maybe so...

TOM   Maybe?

JERRI   I don't know, maybe you're right but...that just feels...like an excuse. You know? (BEAT) It does, like an excuse you make after you lose--like when you come in second. (BEAT) That's what losers do: blame someone.

TOM   I see.

JERRI   I'm not trying to make you mad…

TOM   Ok.

JERRI   I'm not, but…

TOM   I'm not mad…

JERRI   You seem mad.

TOM   I'm not, though…! We just had a difference of opinion, that's all, a BIG one, and I respect that because we just met and that's…BUT if we're ever gonna have any chance of…you know…of this being something--you and I--then we have to be able to point out each other's faults, right? And, and…be able to say 'I'm sorry.' We've gotta be able to talk and joke and just…find some common ground here first before we go forward with any other kind of--

JERRI   Actually, I think we should just call it a night. If that's okay…

TOM   What? I mean…

JERRI   I think I'm gonna go now…

TOM   You're leaving? Wait…no…

JERRI   Yeah…I think you're nice and all that…handsome and a good body… but you're very opinionated and you come on kinda strong when it comes to stuff about 'race' and things, you're quick to take offense when I didn't really-- I mean, you said stuff about my heritage, too, the Crusaders stuff and, and… about the Christians…so…

TOM   I'm a Christian, too! What do you think, I'm a Muslim or something, just because I know who the Moors are? I mean, come on! Seriously!! Don't do this… don't let some stupid…little…disagreement be the end of our--

TOM GOES TO TOUCH JERRI BUT SHE PULLS AWAY THIS TIME, A BIT MORE HARSHLY THAN PERHAPS SHE MEANT TO. TOM IS SURPRISED.

JERRI   NO, STOP! DON'T!! (WAITS A BEAT) Listen, I'm just not looking for anyone like you right now. I just wanna have fun! Meet someone and have fun. Dinner. Sex. Stuff like that. (BEAT) FUN. This…all this…feels too much like work and that's not for me. Not right now--where I am in life.

TOM But...

JERRI Thanks for meeting and good luck. I think you're...very nice, so, be good and, you know...whatever. (BEAT) And by the way, I picked this exhibit to be kind to you...because I thought you might like it...that's why. (BEAT) This was me being thoughtful...

TOM Thoughtful?!! I'm the one being thoughtful here! I've been thoughtful this whole time! I just gave you a pass, Jerri...a HUGE pass on a lotta stuff because, frankly, you said some stupid shit today! You did! I mean, you're just throwing names around and, and you don't know who wrote NATIVE SON or COLOR PUR-PLE or any of that crap!! It's Richard Wright and, and Alice Walker and...come on!!! But I'm still willing to try and make some sort of effort here so the two of us can be--

JERRI Listen, I don't wanna argue with you here, I don't...so no offense and none taken...honestly. (BEAT) Piece of advice, though, if you're gonna keep going after women like me: stop trying so hard...quit being such a know-it-all and just be yourself. It might help... (BEAT) Take care, Tom.

SHE HANDS BACK THE FLOWERS AND WALKS OFF, OUT OF THE GALLERY. TOM STANDS WHERE HE IS, FRUSTRATED AND LOOKING AROUND. CONFUSED BY WHAT'S JUST HAPPENED.

TOM (TO HIMSELF) Yeah...you too...

HE SUDDENLY SMASHES THE FLOWERS ON THE LITTLE TABLE BETWEEN THE BENCHES AND THE PETALS BURST INTO MULTI-COLORED CONFETTI. COVER-ING THE FLOOR. TOM DROPS THE BROKEN STEMS ON A BENCH AND WANDERS OVER TO THE OTHER BENCH AND SITS. SHAKES HIS HEAD. LAUGHS. HE IS ABOUT TO LEAVE BUT SOMETHING ON THE OPPOSITE WALL CATCHES HIS EYE. HE LIFTS HIS HEAD UP TO CONSIDER THE PAINTING. TOM NOW STARES AT THE ARTWORK IN FRONT OF HIM, REALLY TAKING IT IN FOR THE FIRST TIME.

UNLIKELY JAPAN

UNLIKELY JAPAN had its world premiere at the Davenport theater in New York as part of the 'NYC LaBute New Theater Festival' in January 2019. It was directed by Neil LaBute.

Young Woman: Gia Crovatin

Gia Crovatin
Photo: Russ Rowland

A YOUNG WOMAN ON STAGE. TALKING TO US (WHOEVER WE MIGHT BE).

YOUNG WOMAN   ...so this was a while ago, okay? Not that long but a while. A month or two maybe...something like that. Pretty recently. On a weekend, I think...because I had the news on TV, which I never do on the weekdays because I'm not home, I'm working--I manage a bank downtown, a branch, not important but just so you know, I do, and I'm off on Saturdays and Sundays--so it had to be on the weekend. Maybe dinner time...you know, like when you're sitting at the table by yourself or with your family and it's not your usual TV time but the news is on? Just in the background, I mean, it feels fine to have the voices back there talking about world events or the weather or things like that... local or national, doesn't really even matter, it's just the sound of the voices, especially if you're someone who lives alone, sometimes it's nice to hear the sound of another person in the house, that's what I mean. Like that... (BEAT) Anyway...this was after that big thing that happened, over in the...yeah. That shooting. With all the people and the man that was up in the...it was then. Just after that. On the news. I was sitting at home and not really thinking about anything much, just having a salad, kind of an early dinner that I had put togeth- er--not myself but went to one of those places where it's like a big salad bar but somebody else fixes it for you...you point out what you want but they do all the actual making it up and add on the dressing and everything--you can get it on the side, of course, but otherwise they do it for you. The dressing, I'm saying. So yeah, I had one of those for my meal and I was just eating away...staring off into space, and I hear this name. Tim Friedman. I hear that and I look up really quick- ly, while the picture is still there on the screen...just to see if maybe...you know... it's not a common name or anything but it's not crazy-weird, like one that there would only ever be one of...it's not like that, either...there could be others.

SHE STOPS FOR A MOMENT, THINKING ABOUT IT. SHE CONTINUES.

YOUNG WOMAN   You know what I'm saying...you know what I mean. With a name like that...there could be. (BEAT) But no...it's him. The guy they show...this man...he's a man now because it's been quite a few years since I last saw him... but yes. It's Tim. Tim Friedman. Supposedly he was at the thing--not 'supposedly' because he was definitely there, he was in the crowd when it happened and he... he got shot and killed...there weren't many details at the time so I didn't know exactly how he died or how many times the gunman--actually a few people were killed because they were trampled to death...just when the crowd gradually started to realize what was happening they began to move like a giant wave... a few people, a child or two, even, fell and got run over by this...mass of...but he wasn't one of those casualties. Tim wasn't. I learned later that he was shot and killed by the gunman from his vantage point in the tower...the hotel tower where he sprayed bullets down into the crowd. That's how Tim died. (BEAT) I didn't know that at the time, when I saw the news, I mean, I saw that in the story in the TIME magazine I bought or in PEOPLE or one of those things...one of those in-depth features that come out a week or so later when they've got more informa-tion about things..you know, like, with the pictures and illustrations and all that stuff. Maps. I saw it in that, the fact that Tim was one of the...like...forty or fifty people that this man killed with gunfire on that day. I might even be wrong about that--I'm not even sure how many--but a lot. A lot of concert-goers died and so yes, Tim was there. Not 'supposedly' but really there. He was there and he died. (BEAT) And so, like I said, I'm sitting with my salad there...just watching this...and I'm not sad, really, I don't think that's what I feel because it's been so long and we've both done so many things and gone so many places since then, my work and, I dunno, school and, and...the people we've both probably been with by this time--I don't know his story at all, we never stayed in touch so I'm not sure but I'm guessing he must've had a normal amount of...you know... relationships because I certainly have been with a few other guys since then, I'm saying, but I do feel bad...don't get me wrong, I do feel that. Obviously. I feel bad because this person has died, someone that I know...or at least have 'known,' I've known him, in the past, and now he's...dead. Shot dead. So yeah... I don't feel good. I'm not happy about it. I feel bad, but that's different than 'sad.' You see what I mean? It's a very different emotion, I think...and that's what I'm sad about...that I'm not sad. That he and I have drifted so far apart from where we once were that I'm not 'sad' that he's dead; I just feel 'bad,' like if I'd heard that my sister's friend had died, or some forgotten cousin or aunt or whomever, I feel like that, and it happens every day in this country! People are getting shot and killed every-single-day and, and I don't even notice any more, I certainly don't feel bad about it until it's somebody I know...that's how shitty things have gotten...and when that hits me...that's when the tears come. (BEAT) About

10 years ago we were dating...Tim and me...and it got pretty heavy for awhile--and I know, I know, the second I say that and you do the math, you immediately assume that he was my first...the guy who took my virginity or whatever...but that isn't true. It wasn't Tim. Tim thought he did...in fact, I let him think he did, for a long time, that was the story between us, but it wasn't the truth. Someone else did that. (BEAT) But we were still very very close, the two of us, Tim and me, super close and yes, we obviously had sex...many times...and he was a really lovely...just sort of a sweet person, gentle and, I mean, not very experienced, but we were both young and you don't care so much at that age, you just wanna be doing it, with someone you like and who likes you but Hell, you'll accept even less sometimes...lots less...if you're drunk, or, like, horny...you know what I'm saying! You know what I mean...! But yeah...Tim and I were doing that. Being a couple together at school...and having sex...and all that stuff you do at that age. It was pretty normal, like dozens and dozens of other couples. It wasn't that special...no, God, that sounds awful and I don't mean it that way, I'm not being shitty about it, just...honest. It was a regular relationship for two people our age. Just average. Fine. Good times a lot of the time, a few fights but generally we got along and we fit in with our peer group...we were accepted by the others and that's a huge thing at that point, that a person you like is liked by your friends...it was for me, anyway. Still is, I think. Yeah, I mean, yes...why not? Why wouldn't it be? Tim...'Tim'...he ticked a bunch of boxes in my life at that time: he was cute, nice enough body, funny--yeah, a good sense of humor--we shared an Art class and he was easily the top artist in that, which I loved, so yes...he was great...really good. Not quarterback or prom king or a student body president or anything, but a really solid boyfriend and I liked him very much...just in case that was ever in question. In case you're judging me now, about what I say or how I'm saying it...I loved him in a certain way and he loved me too and that's absolutely and one hundred percent true... (BEAT) One thing, though--and this is not a perfect segue, I grant you that--just after saying I loved Tim, but...most of the time I was seeing him, there was someone else in my life as well and Tim, he never knew that. I mean, for awhile he didn't. For a year or so, he had no idea about this other boy...or man, or whatever you'd call him. 'Doug.' He was a year or two ahead of us, graduated already and at community college nearby--living at home but 'in' college and just had a whole different vibe about him. I can't

really explain it, without getting all...it doesn't feel right, to do that at this time, talking mostly about Tim and our...I shouldn't get into the 'Doug' part very much...I just want to be completely open about my history so you can start to understand the sad vs bad thing. So that it makes sense...I mean...the truth'll set you free, right? Isn't that what they say...? (BEAT) Doug was older and had this...he had a beautiful car--shocker, I'm sure--and a job and was studying for his Associates in Criminal-something because he wanted to be a cop, but like a detective, not just a guy on the street...Doug was going to be a real detective, and he was the brother of a friend of my sister and so...you know how this shit happens...it just does. It happens and you go with it or you don't. I did...

SHE TAKES A SIP OF WATER AND THINKS ABOUT WHAT SHE'S SAID SO FAR. AFTER A BEAT, SHE GOES ON:

YOUNG WOMAN Anyway...Tim. This is about him and me and what happened, so...back to Tim. In our senior year, Tim won this photography contest. One that was in a magazine, but a big glossy one, an important Art magazine, and he won it. First prize. With a picture that he took of me. This...well, one that you wouldn't wanna show to your parents or anyone you knew. That kind. I let him take it because he wanted to, really badly--he was always saying how beautiful I was and how great my body was--and so I let him and he promised to never show them around and he was true to that, like, he never showed 'em to his friends or that kind of thing...but he did submit one to this contest...and he won. And he got paid a lot of money...I mean, what seemed like a lot, anyhow, for back then. We couldn't tell anyone and we both sat through the whole month--it was the MARCH issue, I can still remember that, when it was published--hoping no one we knew would see it or buy it or...thirty days we waited! So shit-scared that we bought up the two copies that they got at Barnes & Noble...and that wasn't even in town, that was at the mall about twenty minutes away...we bought both of 'em just in case...March came and went and nobody ever had a clue. It was our secret, Tim and I. Not that you could tell it was me in the picture, the way that I was lying on the bed...with just my...but yeah, we kept that secret to this day. Just the two of us. And with his earnings, the check he got from the magazine contest, he made plans for us to go away together on a trip, that's how far along this thing had gotten with him...our relationship...and I liked him, I totally did, I've told you that already, but like I said...I was also seeing this Doug guy as well. Not in public or anything...we were not 'dating' is what I'm saying to you...but at his place. You know. Obviously you know what I'm saying. You know what I mean...

SHE TAKES A BREATH AND LETS US CATCH UP. WHEN WE DO:

YOUNG WOMAN Right? You understand the delicacy of the situation I was in, the spot I had put myself in. That's how my Grandma would say it, 'Oh sweetie, you've got yourself in a real spot. In a real bad spot.' Grandma would say that if she was still alive now or had known about it at that time, and she'd be right. I was...I was in a terrible spot. Tim had used his earnings to buy us two tickets overseas--for the trip I mentioned--he went ahead and got us two seats going to Japan, which, to be fair, he never asked me if I was okay with that, I mean, beyond the general plan to go away on some kind of vacation together, Tim had not checked with me first about the specifics of it. Japan is far! It's a long ways away and he got them for a week that was...I'm not just, you know, making excuses, I'm not...he really should've asked me first but he didn't, he bought them as a kind of surprise graduation thingie and so when he told me...what could I say? I mean...I sorta had to say 'yes,' didn't I? I thought so, and I did, at the time. I told him I'd go, that I was happy and excited to go with him...but not really. I already had plans that week and it was with Doug and I know I said that it wasn't a big deal, whatever was going on between us, Doug and myself--and it wasn't, I swear that it was not, not really--but we were gonna go to this concert that was in Chicago, a big three-day thing with a bunch of bands I liked and so... yes. At that age I wanted to do that more than I wanted to see Japan. Sorry but it was just kind of...unlikely...the idea of me in Japan and Tim was the one who was so fascinated by the place, not me, he wanted me to be but it was just him really--and Japan is cool, it totally is, their culture and the people and all that-- Anime!--but to be fair, I never asked to go there. (BEAT) I was also kind of what- ever, I was worried that Tim might be getting really serious about us and bring a ring or something like that...that he might turn to me as we're standing by some fish pond or one of those things--what're they even called? Pagodas, I think... one of those and get down on his knee and do that. Some...shit...like that which I wouldn't be ready for and that would ruin the whole trip if I said 'no'....so...I just...

SHE PAUSES AT THIS, LOOKING OUT AT US. QUIET. FINALLY:

YOUNG WOMAN   I didn't say anything...at all. I just smiled and nodded and listened to Tim as he made plans for us...he bought one of those guidebooks and would read things out loud when we were together at dinner or over at one of our places...I still lived with my parents at that point but he had his own place... with a few other people. An apartment. Both his parents had passed away in a car accident so he lived with his grandmother when he was younger but he got some money from insurance and he moved out in high school. So...when we were in his room he would be making lists of things for us to see and do and places to eat, seven days all laid out and with not very much input from me. He wasn't mean about it, just kind of bossy...like he knew what we should do and what I would like. Acting that way...like guys do. (BEAT) But the day of...when we were supposed to leave, I knew I wasn't going and I knew what that would mean for us as a couple...I knew all that...but I guess I kinda wanted it to end, right? I mean, I must've wanted that. You don't come back from a thing like that; I left him standing there at the airport, trying my phone over and over and wondering what could be going on--he even called the house phone but I forbid my mom to pick it up, I FORBID her to--and I think at the final moment there, when they were calling for the last people to get on board...he knew I wasn't hurt or injured or that something bad had happened. No. He knew. He got it, right there at the gate...that I was standing him up...that I was fine and had made a choice and not even bothered to tell him, I just left him there looking stupid and went on about my life. (BEAT) It was a shitty thing to do...there is no question about it...but it's the kind of thing you do at an age like that, that's how you take care of things. Badly. Stupidly. Fuck it up and walk away like it never even happened...step up and over the pile of shit you've made and that's what I did. Which is how Tim played it, too, when he got back. Never said a word about it to me...never called me again--we were graduated by then so he didn't really have to see me if he didn't want to--and Tim did not want to. He never spoke about his trip--not just to me but to anyone, I don't think, not that I ever heard--he just acted like it never happened. The trip. Us. None of it. (BEAT) I went off to college a few months later and we lost touch...like people can do...even people who don't want to or swear they won't do...so imagine how easy it was for us to do that. Doug and I also fizzled out, I mean, I knew that was gonna happen, even before it started I knew that...but it was fun for awhile and the concert was great, so...

I can't complain much. (LAUGHS) That's a nice name for it, by the way, what happened to Tim and me. We 'lost touch.' You know what that means. Tim didn't speak to me again and I never had the guts to track him down or look him in the eye...or let him know that I was very very sorry for what I'd done. That it was bad and I was an idiot and have thought about it so many times in my life since then. I...didn't do that and that's...well, you know what that means... (BEAT) And then there I am, years later, seeing his photo on the news, looking into the camera but not smiling--Tim never smiled in pictures--and I see that he died.

HER EYES WELL UP WITH TEARS BUT SHE RESISTS CRYING.

YOUNG WOMAN   At some sort of concert, listening to a kind of music I never had any idea that he even liked--maybe he didn't when I knew him, I dunno-- but he was dead and it made me feel bad about it...even worse when I found out later that he was an artist, a painter who was pretty successful--known for his nudes, actually...these photo-realistic nudes that he did and looked very very much like a picture that he'd taken of a girl back in high school who never loved him enough. *Yeah.* (BEAT) All during that meal when I first found out that he'd died, and through most of whenever...I keep wondering if what I did, any of it, put Tim on a path that finally led him to that place. To that show and to that evening. I mean, after all, he was there in town at an art show, selling his work, so...who knows? I don't...maybe. I suppose. Probably. Also probably not... but there is that possibility that if I'd not done what I did...if we'd gone to Japan, if he'd knelt there under a cherry tree and given me a ring--or even if that part didn't take place, the ring part, if we'd just gone together on that vacation...however unlikely that scenario was at that point in my life...then he might've been sitting across from me that night at dinner as we watched the news and heard about those horrible events of that awful, terrible day. OR I might've been there with him near the stage, holding a plate of bar-b-que in my hands and smiling at him while we listened to that same band, tapping our feet to those same rhythms, and I too might've been gunned down that night, or trampled by a crowd or taken to the hospital and died. It's possible...very very possible. (BEAT) Is that what my life was meant to be, instead of what it is today? Is it? Anyway...I just wanted to say it, to get it out and let you know... I'm not asking for your...doesn't matter now. It's happened...it's over...you know what I'm saying. You know what I mean. (BEAT) Look, in the grand scheme of things, who can say or see or ever really know? If I was right or wrong in what I did...or am I just a person, doing what we always do? Stumbling forward through our lives, trying our best, sometimes failing, sometimes not...until we reach the end of it all--the very bitter end. (BEAT) I don't know. (BEAT) Do you? (BEAT) Do you have the answers to all that...to *any* of it? (BEAT) I'll tell you what: you're lucky if you do, because I don't...I never have...and I probably never will.

SHE TRIES TO SMILE BUT JUST MISSES IT. SHE STARES AT US.

SAINT LOUIS

*SAINT LOUIS had its world premiere at the Gaslight Theater as part of
the 'LaBute New Theater Festival' in St. Louis Missouri in July 2022.
It was directed by Spencer Sickmann.*

Scott: Brock Russell
Stephanie: Carly Uding
Sue: Bryn McLaughlin

*(left to right) Carly Uding, Brock Russell, Bryn McLaughlin
Photo: Patrick Huber*

THERE THEY ARE. ALL THREE OF THEM. STANDING SEPARATELY. THE REST OF THE SPACE IS EMPTY, EXCEPT FOR A SMALL CIRCLE OF LIGHT OVER EACH PERSON, SPILLING ONTO THE FLOOR TO CREATE THREE POOLS OF BRIGHT-NESS IN THE DARK.

HIM ...this is...I don't even know why I'm telling you this...it's really none of your business.

HER Who told you about this? Did Sue? Seriously, was it her? I'm curious.

SHE You didn't hear it from me, I'm not that kind of person, who needs to spill all my private stuff around so everybody else can wallow in it. I don't do that...

HIM This was years ago, anyway, so it's not that big a thing, I mean, I can barely remember 'em, who they were, what they looked like...

HER It seems like it was yesterday...

HIM Alright, that's not completely true because I obviously remember what they looked like, both of 'em. The one named Stephanie, who was just incredible looking--I mean, beautiful--and then the other one, too, who was pretty as well but just a little bit more--you know what I'm saying! I don't wanna say dyke-ish or a phrase like that because it's not nice, but...how about 'serious' instead? She was the more 'serious-looking' of the two. Anyway, yes...I obviously do remember 'em both.

SHE A lot of this happened without me being directly involved...or even know-ing about it, for that matter, so 'no'....I can't just immediately pull it up and give you details...sorry, but I can't.

HIM She also had an edge, too, did I say that already? No? Well, yeah, she did... the other one. 'Sue.' (USES AIR QUOTES) Ha! Not sure why I just did that, used 'air' quotes because that's her name, Sue, not 'Sue,' which would imply that I'm saying 'Sue' but meaning something else and I'm not...that's her actual name... not her 'name.' (USES AIR QUOTES) I think I do that a lot, which is funny. Not funny ha-ha but, you know...funny stupid. (USES AIR QUOTES) 'Funny.'

HER I'm trying to remember now if we met on the street first or in the hallway downstairs...down where the mail boxes are...it might've been there. (THINKING)

Ummmmmmm...

HIM She wasn't mean or anything like that...not outright in your face like some people can be--women of that type, I'm saying--but pushy about the 'gay' thing, how she felt about men in general...so that kinda put me off a bit.

SHE People are so easily offended by honesty, which is...what do you want me to say to that? (SHRUGS) Sorry? (QUOTING) What did Shakespeare say? "Truth is truth to the end of reckoning..."

HIM They were already there when I...you know...when I moved into the building. That much I remember...

SHE He said that? That we were already there? And so what if we were? Does that make this our fault or something...does it? (WAITS) I am not arguing with you...I'm asking.

HIM I'm not saying anything at all...all I said was I know they were in their apartment before I was ever a tenant there...I don't know why that's, like, a contentious thing. It's the truth, so, I'm sorry if that's annoying but it is what it is--it's the truth--and no amount of subjective bullshit is gonna change that.

HER We were definitely there first...

HIM They had a 2 bedroom apartment on the third floor, very nice and also on this side-- (INDICATES) --so extra windows and a nice Eastern light in the mornings; it was a very choice spot and so...yeah...I remember it well. I don't see how that can be a 'thing' with them...or with one of 'em anyway--lemme guess who? Gee, I wonder--but whatever. That's how it was, go look up their lease or talk to the landlord if you wanna, but I know what I'm talking about here: they lived there before I did...end of story.

HER We've had the place for almost all the time that we've been together, which is nearly...God...nine years next Fall. Damn, that's crazy, is it THAT long? (THINKS) Yeah, must be...we've been a couple for just about nine years now. Shit. Wow.

SHE It's a serious, committed relationship. (BEAT) On my part, at least.

HER   We've even talked about children but that's a whole...you know...do I really wanna get into this right now...? We didn't have an obvious donor we both agreed on, or some guy who was ready to help us out, so that's...you know...and the cost of going to a fertility specialist is astronomical--it was for us, anyway-- so it just wasn't very feasible right then...

SHE   Obviously this was an ongoing discussion with us...'children'...

HIM   Anyway, I'd always liked that building, the times I'd driven past it. It was this Art Deco-looking place over on Maryland and so...yeah...I kind of always kept my eye out for any apartments that might open up in there. (BEAT) That is absolutely true...

SHE   He lived downstairs from us for I'm not even sure how long...must be at least a year. I think. Six months? I don't know...

HER   The building was divided into eight apartments, two on each floor, so it was a really nice layout with a lot of windows and a central staircase that kind of...you know-- (AS SHE INDICATES) --what am I trying to say? It put a natural... space between you and your neighbor...whomever you shared a floor with, so on top of everything else it was nice and quiet, which for me was great because I work from home...

HIM   I think she was an illustrator of some kind, that's what she told me, for either magazines or books...or maybe both. Did she do both? Seems like it. (BEAT) They had a lot of her work--framed and hung up, I mean...like actual 'art'-- in their apartment. (SMILES) She was really good. Impressive.

HER   Did he say that? That he liked my work? (SMILES) That's sweet...

SHE   Steph is an incredible artist...graphic designer...anything visual and she can do it. So proud of her.

HIM   The other one...the you-know-what one...I think she was also in the arts or something. A writer, I was told...playwright or something...she talked like she was, anyway, alway quoting books and movies.

SHE   "If this were played upon a stage now I could condemn it as an improbable fiction..."

HIM   *(USES AIR QUOTES)* ...'whatever'...

SHE   I'm a playwright, yes, that's true, but I also direct and I'm an educator as well, so...yeah...I'm a little more than just a 'writer.'

HIM   She's definitely thought very highly of herself, I'll give her that. (LAUGHS) Anyway, I'm just messing around, ok? I'm just being silly; I could care less what she did...

HER   Needless to say, Scott and Sue did not exactly 'hit it off.'

HIM   I tried and that's the truth...! I absolutely tried to be friendly with her but she was not having it, at all...plus she said some shit about me, behind my back, or what she thought was behind my back, early on and that really kinda pissed me off...you know? I was like...'ummmm, excuse me, *Ellen*, but where the fuck do you get off making fun of anybody?' Right? I mean, seriously. (BEAT) What? No, Jesus, oh course not...I'd never say that out loud...no!! I don't even mean 'Ellen,' anyway, I'm not talking about the real one, the lady on the show, be-cause she actually comes off kinda nice most of the time...I'm talking about her girlfriend or her wife or whatever. You know who I mean...the blonde; the way women like that--the pretty ones--can act sometimes or have that look...what do they call 'em...'lipstick lesbians?' Yeah, those ones. Like they know everything.

HER   I'm not even sure what she said that started it...something like, I dunno... I think she called him 'the white nightmare' one time or something close to that...

SHE   It was a joke...

HIM   Trust me, this was NOT a joke...

SHE   It was nothing! It was in reference to something Steph said when he did her a favor of some kind...helped her with the door or carried the groceries for her or some sorta...I can't even remember now...

HER   I called him a 'white knight,' is what started it all...

SHE   Ugh.

HER   What's the matter with that?

HIM   They were arguing about it and I could hear it through the floor, that's what happened...

SHE   And I said something like 'yeah, 'white night-mare' is more like it...something stupid like that.

HIM   It wasn't stupid, it was mean.

SHE   What is he, like, six years old? THAT hurt his feelings...it was a pun! And a bad one at that...I'm not even sure it is a pun!

HIM   Whatever...she's a bitch. Honestly, she is. She was always saying derogatory stuff about me. (BEAT) I mean it. Ask Stephanie.

HER   Meaning he was everything that she disliked about men: white, good-looking, straight...and this sense of just--you know what I'm talking about--this way of walking around with a smile on his face, like he was better than everyone...like he owned the place.

HIM   Who said that? I never said that...

HER   Not that it felt that way or he acted like that--not around me, anyway--but it was the way he looked at you, that's what really got under Sue's skin, just the look on his face... (BEAT) Obviously it didn't bother me.

SHE   *Obviously...*

HIM   I didn't do anything to that girl! Seriously...nothing. I was nothing but nice, any time I saw her. Just smiled and went about my business.

SHE   He was an asshole...and that's not just me talking, I promise you. It isn't. A lot of my friends felt the same way; not for anything specific that he did--not at first, anyway--but just because of who he was and how he was and whatever else he did or said or--listen, I don't really wanna get back into all this, actually, so let's just leave it at that. Ok?

HIM   Doesn't matter...this stuff doesn't have anything to do with the whole rest of the story...not really. I mean, it doesn't help that she and I couldn't stand each other--Sue, I mean--but I think Stephanie and I might've, you know, still gone through what we did together if Sue hadn't been in the picture...who knows for sure, but still, I think it's possible, very possible that we would've met and had some kind of...whatever you wanna call it...a connection between us either way.

HER   I absolutely did like him, kind of right from the beginning. I'm not gonna deny that, because then I'd be lying to you. Yes, I was living with Sue, yes, we were in a relationship--I mean, we obviously had a few problems of our own, that's pretty obvious, but still--so, yes, I kind of had no business letting it happen, whatever happened, but I wanna be completely clear right up front about all this: I don't blame anyone else for my feelings or the events of that summer...I honestly do not... (BEAT) I'm as responsible for what went on as much as anybody...certainly as much as he was. Scott. I know Sue wants you to believe something other than that, but it's just...no, that's not the truth. It just isn't.

HIM   I'll tell you what...she certainly didn't have a 'type.' Stephanie, I mean. 'Sue.' Me. That's like...wow. Big difference there...!

HER   I like who I like...that's not even anything worth discussing. God. I'm into people, individuals...not just looks. Legs or tits or whatever...muscles. I like PEO-PLE. I like men and women and I've dated both, never based on any one thing, never just about sex or looks or personality. (SHRUGS) I like who I like, which is totally alright. Isn't it?

HIM   I had no problem with it whatsoever...I'm just pointing it out, that's all. (BEAT) Her taste was all over the map...

SHE   I'm a very...monogamous person and I always have been, so when Steph has shown interest in other people, that's not easy...I'd be lying if I said differently. It hurts my feelings...how could it not? Right? She swears it's not about anything, not meant to hurt us, but...you know...how does that work? I'm just gonna look the other way and act like her and somebody else together is no big deal, even if it's just once, for *dinner?* That's impossible...

HIM   I remember the first time I spoke to Stephanie, at the building, I didn't even live there yet. I was there to meet an agent from this service that I use, and they were late, and I was just standing at the gate, waiting for 'em or to get buzzed in or something, and Stephanie walks toward me from along the sidewalk, carrying her bags and a little bit flushed...

HER   This is probably around March or something like that, the beginning of spring...but it might've been a little later, too...like...

SHE   It was March. Definitely March.

HIM   And I jump in to try and help her as she's juggling bags of groceries-- not plastic ones, I remember that very specifically, because she had her own bags which were nicer and a bit sturdier, the kind you pay more for but they're canvas or woven or whatever and you bring 'em along to a store with you--and she's trying to find her keys so I offer to hold the bags for her. (BEAT) It was no big deal...I would've done that for anybody. (SMILES) Well, almost anybody-- read into that what you will.

SHE   I think he went out of his way sometimes to make noise downstairs, and I mean that...out of his way. With his records and DEADPOOL movies and his talking loud on the phone, even late at night--it's an older house and it's got thick walls and all that but sound travels right through the floor and ceiling.... and he knew that. I told him so, many times...so, yeah...he knew.

HER   It was very nice of him to grab my groceries and help me out, that's something you're taught or you're not, at a very early age, it's not a thing that everybody does. It's not, believe me...

HIM   Trust me, she played music, too...and movies and all kinds of stuff. This 'lezzy' stuff--and that's not me being rude or judgemental--I'm simply reporting facts. If I ever asked what was on or who was singing or anything like that: it was always FOUR NON-BLONDES or MAZZY STAR or THE 'L' WORD...something called DESERT HEARTS...ever hear of a movie called THE FOX? It's about two 'lady friends' who have a guy move onto their farm...and in the end one of 'em shoots him. *Nice.* Or how about a movie called THE KILLING OF SISTER GEORGE? (WAITS) Yeah, me either, not until I moved into that building. THE CHILDREN'S HOUR and BLUE IS THE WARMEST COLOR--is it really? I don't know about that--but on and on and on, it was always gay-themed, whatever Sue watched and that's fine, go for it, live-and-let-live but...I mean...alright already... you can't just watch GONE WITH THE WIND one time...? Or WIZARD OF OZ? Something else just once without it having to have 'two women in love living in a world that doesn't understand them and yet on they go, taking care of each other and fighting to be together and...' blah-blah-blah. (BEAT) You know what I mean, right? Why because you're gay can you only watch or listen to or discuss gay stuff? I watch gay stuff, too--BROKEBACK MOUNTAIN and, ummm, whatever...other ones, too...but I mix it up...that's just normal, isn't it, to mix things up once in awhile? Some GAME OF THRONES one night--which also has some gay parts in it--and then a football game another night, a comedy or whatnot when you've got a girl over or friends--I don't mean the show FRIENDS, which I watch, too, or WILL & GRACE, which is, like, super-gay and I've watched that many times--those actors on it are fucking funny, they really are--BUT it's not just constant, like Sue is with her stuff. What is it, I wonder? That need to be so uber-gay? Like she's gonna get kicked outta the club if she isn't just endlessly pushing the agenda or something. (SHRUGS) I dunno, but I'm certainly not gonna ask her and I don't even live there now so it's no big thing...you brought it up earlier so I'm just answering you about it. Okay? (BEAT) Okay, good. (BEAT) Did I mention she's black? So there's that, too.

HER   She can be a little intense...

SHE   I know he talked about me behind my back all the time...I know he did. Steph even told me he did.

HER   The time I spent with Scott I made sure that Sue was off-limits...

HIM   We didn't really talk about her...'Sue'--welterweight champion of the world--I'm kidding...I mean, am I? Do I think she'd actually punch me if we got into it? Yeah, probably...not that she could take me--in a fair fight, I'm saying--but the fact that I'm even considering it, weighing my chances...should tell you a lot about Sue. Right? (BEAT) Anyhow, yeah...she would come up occasionally in conversation but not because I was being mean or anything like that; if it came up at all it was Steph doing it first...complaining about their relationship or how controlling she could be or stuff like that so don't let her tell you different. Sue, I mean, not Steph. Well, either one of them...actually...from what I could see they had a ton of shit going on between 'em and that had nothing to do with me or Stephanie and me or any of that...that was just life stuff and so whatever happened between us had nothing to do with them. (BEAT) Does that make any sense? (BEAT) I hope so.

SHE   I'm not being dramatic when I say that he almost ruined our lives...both our lives, hers and mine, and our life together so, yes, I don't have great things to say about him. Obviously not. (BEAT) Sorry.

HIM   No, that's not dramatic at all...nope. (BEAT) I mean...unbelievable, that one. (BEAT) 'SUE.'

HER   Anything that happened was just us and life and not...Sue gets very grandiose and that's just part of who she is and what I love about her, too, but, no...Scott did not ruin anybody's life...I can look you in the eye and say that...I mean it, directly in the eye and say 'no, that is not true.'

SHE   Bullshit.

HIM   I'm not a finger-pointer, so...whatever they've said about it is how they feel and that's valid and fine but I take responsibility for me and that's it. Ok? Fair enough? (WAITS) Was that a pretty successful dodge of actually answering the question? (LAUGHS) Yeah, I thought so! Good! Job well done...

HER   We started seeing each other...that's what happened, so, call it anything you want to but that's the truth: Scott and I started seeing each other...behind Sue's back...which happens sometimes in life, it does, and there's no use trying to blame someone or...just...

SHE   I wasn't sure what was going on...not for quite a while...

HER   I just said that, right? It feels like we're going in circles here...

HIM   I moved in and then, yeah...it was pretty soon after that when we began to...I dunno...hook up or get together--I wouldn't exactly call it 'dating' but--there was a fair amount of sneaking up and down the stairs and phone calls and fucking at my place or their place or...I mean, how specific do I need to be about all that for you here?

SUE   Yeah, it got pretty serious, from what Steph's told me about it...which might not be everything, to be honest...I think she might be holding some things back from me, even to this day...

HIM   I never said a word...

HER   Look, she does not need to know every last detail...that's...no one does. Honestly, it's...I'm not cool with that. (BEAT) Some of that's just...pure...gossip, you know what I mean...? It just is, even if it's your own partner, the ONLY reason they've got for wanting to hear some of that stuff is just purely...it's not helpful! Who's got a bigger this or was she a better that than me...? Shit like that will ruin you, it will destroy you as a couple, I promise you it will...and I, for one, am not willing to go there, no matter if Sue or Scott or whomever we're talking about wants to engage in that. No, I won't...I just will not do it...

SUE   That summer I had a fellowship to work in Ashland, at the Shakespeare Festival there...which was just a HUGE thing for me and...a very...it was big...and so I was gonna be gone for, like, four months...which is a long time to be away from someone, and we'd agreed for me to take it, no question that I was gonna do it, but we also talked about her coming out there with me, since her work is fairly mobile and that would've been really nice and fun and...and yes, hindsight is 20/20 or however that saying goes but we did talk about it...that's all that I wanna point out here...is that we did discuss it, we did, we made some plans... and...we did.

HER   Sue talked about it, yes, she did, definitely true, but that's not the same as 'talking about it,' which we didn't do...*she* talked about it, *she* begged me to do it, *she* bullied me about it many times but I never once said 'yes, that's great, I'll go with you to Oregon.' Not once.

SUE   Untrue...

HER   True...

HIM   I have no idea.

SHE   Why would I say that if it wasn't true...I mean...why?!

HER   Believe what you want.

HIM   Her girlfriend went off to some Shakespreare...camp...or whatever. (BEAT) 'Camp?' (USES AIR QUOTES) I think so...yeah...I'm not sure! Something to do with Shakespeare...people acting shit out. I dunno.

SHE   Trust me, she agreed to come out there with me...at least once if not several times...

HIM   Sometimes conversations came down through those old-timey vents, you know the kind I mean? The rectangle kind with the grating in the wall, and I could overhear some stuff and I vaguely remember a few talks that had to do with Shakespeare or the West Coast or something like that; I'm not taking sides or trying to protect anybody, either one of 'em, by me saying that...but it's true.

SHE   Doesn't matter...in the end I went.

HER   Four months. (BEAT) Her choice.

HIM   And so...obviously...Stephanie is suddenly around by herself a lot more at this point and...you know...it's summer and it's St. Louis and it's muggy and she's wearing all these cute little tops and shorts or those clingy dresses that girls like to wear in the summertime...she looked amazing.

HER   I really wasn't trying to force anything to happen...absolutely not. It was summer. It was hot. People try and stay cool, that's all it was...me trying to stay cool. I did not lead him on...

HIM   I'm not saying a word...

SHE   I said 'I wouldn't put it past her' that's what I said. (BEAT) I don't think that's a derogatory statement or unkind or anything. I don't...telling the truth is not mean! It's the truth, that's all it is. It's me being honest...how can that be mean?

HIM   Plus we just got along...as people, I'm saying. We clicked and laughed and we talked about stuff, agreed on restaurants and shows, lots of things...so why wouldn't we hang out together? Sometimes just out on their porch or mine, or watching a movie or walking around the neighborhood...like I said before, we didn't really 'date,' that is not what happened...it was friendly and casual... but, yes...it got a little outta hand...by the end.

HER   Please don't ask me for specifics because I'm not gonna do that...

HIM   You've seen her, so you know what her body's like...incredible...but honestly, I liked the person, too, and not just...you know...

SHE   We were doing a summer of romance plays, which...looking back...that was very fucking ironic. Classics and some new pieces as well, commissions, all of them based around the general theme of 'love.'

HIM   ... (SHRUGS)

HER   I ultimately didn't go out to see anything like we discussed, but I think that's...there was a bunch of factors that determined that decision...money, mostly...

SHE   Steph had talked to me about seeing TAMING OF THE SHREW because I was the dramaturg on that production and we were doing some interesting things with the setting--and race and class and a bunch of stuff--and it's just one of those texts in the canon that we've discussed and argued over many times, Sue and I...

HER   MANY times...

HIM   No, I've never read it...what's it called again? TAMING OF THE SHREW, is that it? Yeah, I've heard of it before, of course, but never read it, not in school or as an assignment or anything. (BEAT) I did see ROMEO + JULIET on TV... the DiCaprio one? (BEAT) 's good. (BEAT) Lot of fun.

HER   I actually see what Petruchio's up to in that story, which is not the most popular opinion of the year...and I don't mean everything he does or...I just think Katherine brings a lot of that shit on herself. It's true. (BEAT) Let's not get into it, alright? It's just an opinion...

SHE   But she never made the trip...

HER   I don't really wanna talk about this any more...is that alright?

HIM   And it was just this...I dunno...this amazing summer we had. That's all. Amazing. I really liked her...you know? Obviously I knew what the situation was, going into it, and I had no sense of, of...expectation, I guess...that I was gonna step in and sweep her off her feet and we'd run off into the sunset together... but hey...shit happens, right? Sometimes it does and it was possible. I mean, anything's possible...she told me herself that she's dated guys before and so that's...all I'm saying is that I wasn't just doing it to get at Sue...no way...not at all. It was never just that.

HER We have an open relationship, I've already gone over all that...

SHE OPEN is not a word that we've ever used in conversation together, but if she called it that to you then I guess that's what we have...

HER Oh, come on, please...

HIM Ok, yeah, spoiler alert! Did I like her and think for a couple seconds there that maybe we could make it work out and could I see us as a couple, together, and without Uncle Sue in the picture? Yes! Of course I could...why not? We had a thing between us, a whatever, and we...just...we looked good together, we fit, you know? Unlike Stephanie and somebody I know...hint, hint...and I'm not being judgemental--says the guy who's about to be judgemental--but I know you know what I mean. Of course you do.

HER I've heard this before, about Sue and myself...about our compatibility or whatever...and I think it's so shitty, to judge people like that. Who is anyone to say if we make a good couple or not? I mean, what's a 'good couple,' anyway...? Seriously...what? I'd love to know if you've got the answers...

HIM All I mean is...you pass two sets of couples on the street: one, you glance at 'em and they look good together and on you go with your day, doesn't bother you at all...and the other one, because of whatever it is--age or gender or looks, any number of things but it just catches your eye--and it's obvious that they don't belong together...it's not you, it's the universe...they-do-not-fit. One of 'em's amazing and the other one's...really fucking lucky. (SMILES) Right?

HER She's not even--Sue put on a little weight after college...I mean, so what? She lost most of it again. *Most.*

SHE Has she dated other people in nine years? I said 'yes' before. Have we spent time apart during our life together? 'Yes' again. Point is: we are still connected...still here...still a couple...so, I'm not sure what you're getting at...

HIM And then...suddenly--or that's how it seemed anyway--things changed. Later it all kinda made sense, the timing and all that, that we were getting to the end of the summer--end of the fellowship for BIG SUE--and so things started to taper off with Stephanie all of a sudden... (BEAT) She'd say she didn't feel well after we'd made plans, eight o'clock in the morning and she's suddenly got the flu or whatever, throwing up and canceling a lunch or, like, too tired to watch tv after talking about it all day...just 'things.' Things that became so obvious when I put it together but for a few weeks there I really felt like an idiot, not under-standing that this was her way of saying goodbye and I just kept going back, banging my head on her door like a puppy dog, thinking that 'this time she's gonna open it...well, surely this time she's gonna open it...' until it sort of got to be a bit embarrassing for both of us and after that--after I figured it out--I then graciously backed out of the situation...'graciously?' No, that isn't right... (THINKS) I mean 'gracefully.' Yeah. That.

HER   We just sort of stopped seeing each other when Fall rolled around is what happened...there wasn't any big dramatic ending or whatever. Did he say there was or something? Because that's not true...

SHE   I actually don't know all the ins and outs of how things tapered off but I'm sure it was Steph who ended it...that was just her way...

HIM   What I said was I was the one who technically 'ended' it because of how she was treating me right before we hit Labor Day.

HER   Okay, well, that's different...

HIM   We were gonna go to a Cardinals game--which sounded kinda fun but then, yeah, I guess she felt 'sick' again or...I got a voicemail from her but I barely listened to it...same old thing she'd been doing for almost all of August so I was like, 'fuck it...' and I went by myself. It was bobble-head night and I saw some friends of mine and so I got to sit way closer than I would've with the tickets I already had...so. (BEAT) It was fun.

HER   Scott didn't renew his lease...

HIM   I had a 6 month thing there and in the end, it's an old building--they keep it up, especially on the outside so it looks good for passersby and potential rent-ers--but you have to pay all the utilities and, you know, the rooms are small... plus with what had happened between us, Stephanie and me--and I knew she was gonna tell Sue about it, I mean, 100 percent they're gonna hash that shit out and I can just imagine listening to that, night after night through the ceiling and Sue running down and knocking on my door or...worse...she catches me in the stairwell and attacks me with some sort of a lesbian...weapon...or whatever! (INDICATES) Slits my throat with the jagged edge of a Tracy Chapman album or something so I was, like, 'ummmmmm, no thank you'...and so I got outta there... cleaned the place up and collected my deposit and got a nice two-bedroom in this new building over in Shrewsbury.

SHE   I got back in town on the 5th...

HER   We never really got a chance to say 'goodbye' or anything like that...which is pretty much my fault, because of the way I treated him at the end...but it was never meant to be...some...I was not going to leave Sue or what we had, not for someone who was...Scott was very nice and he could be hilarious, when you got to know him, we had a really great couple months together, but that's not... (BEAT) I feel like you want me to say 'I'm sorry' or that I had some sort of plan in mind and that's not, I'm not even gonna dignify that...seriously, I'm not going to. (BEAT) I don't have anything to be sorry for, I'm not ashamed, so...that's how I'm gonna leave it. We can stand here all day or do whatever you wanna do but I am not gonna give you some big revelation to finish things off; it happened...we had our time...and life went on.

HIM   But no, I don't think she used me any more than I did her. Why, did someone say that? (BEAT) Never saw them again, actually, either one of 'em...which is normal, I guess, for a city. Cities are funny like that, right? Funny weird, I mean. Big ones, anyway. New York, Chicago, even a place like here. St. Louis. (BEAT) You run into people you haven't seen in years twice in one day and another person...you live next to 'em your whole childhood and after they go off to school you never see 'em again. 30 years later, at some funeral...you realize they only moved six blocks away and you've been this close to each other all that time. (USES HANDS TO INDICATE HOW FAR AWAY) Anyway, yeah...I moved out.

SHE   "Exit, pursued by a bear."

HER   Somebody in our building, an older man who lived on the first floor-- this was a few years later--came upstairs and showed us an obituary in the POST-DISPATCH and it was him. (BEAT) 'Scott.'

SHE   He was hit by a garbage truck over on Chippewa. (BEAT) No comment.

HIM   I went right through a red light...it was my own fucking fault. (BEAT) 'Mostly.' (USES AIR QUOTES)

SHE   We recognized his photo when that guy from downstairs showed it to us. It was him, for sure.

HER   It wasn't a very good picture but it was definitely him and we were both... even Sue cried about it...something so senseless like that. (BEAT) We took our daughter with us to the memorial...she was three by that point and very sweet and we just decided that it was the right thing to do, to take her with us.

SHE   I was out-voted...

HER   They had a very nice service for him at the church he grew up in...out in Bartlesville.

SHE   And we never talked about him again after that...not by name, at least.

HER   I'm sorry...who did you *think* the father was? (BEAT) It was Scott. We still live there, in that same building...all these years later. Our daughter goes to school a few blocks away and so...we're...

SHE   Things are good.

HER   Things are fine.

SHE   "The rest is silence."

HER   I guess. Most times, if you said that to me--You good? You getting by?-- I'd probably smile and agree with you. I do love Sam. Our little girl. She's every-thing to me. (BEAT) Everything.

HIM   I drove by there one time, just one time, I swear--I'm not like a lame stalker dude or anything--but I was 'in the neighborhood' as they say, don't even remember when, this had to be, like, a few months or even longer, a year, maybe...after all that shit went down with the, you know...moving out and the virus and the...all of that stuff...God, just so much stuff! (BEAT) And I guess I just wanted to see if they were ok...check if they were still even living there...

I turned down the street and went past the building, just to see...not hoping I'd get a peek at her or anything, get one last glance at Stephanie or some stupid shit like that...but just, you know...just to see... (BEAT) OK! So I sort of waited a little bit...down the block...Jesus, so what? Parking is shit over there, that's one more reason I didn't up my lease again...but I could see the house and all that in my side mirror...and for a minute there I thought that I saw 'em again...both of them...walking down the street with their masks on and a bunch of grocery bags. Of course! Ha! Them with their groceries--and holding hands as they headed back from the store.

SHE   After all, we're a family now...no matter what.

HER   The three of us....

HIM   It was sunny and bright and I had the light in my eyes and so I'm not sure...but in the end I think it was some other couple...still two ladies but not them because they had a baby with 'em...the one I thought was Stephanie (meaning the pretty one)--I'm kidding!--she was carrying what looked to me like a beautiful little girl in one of those carriers across her chest...so it must've been somebody else, I guess...living in that same house. (BEAT) Afterwards I drove off and went back to my place...the new one I told you about.

SHE   A happy little family.

HER   I guess so. I guess that's what we are. (BEAT) Aren't we?

HIM   It's funny, right? How your mind can play tricks on you like that: make you see things that were never really there. Well...I think it is, anyway. (BEAT) It's funny. (BEAT) I mean, not 'funny ha-ha' but...you know...

POOLS OF LIGHT FADE OUT, ONE AFTER THE NEXT AFTER THE NEXT. LIKE MEMORIES, VANISHING INTO THE DISTANCE. ONE-TWO-THREE.

SAFE SPACE

SAFE SPACE had its world premiere at the Gaslight Theater as part of the 'LaBute New Theater Festival' in St. Louis Missouri in July 2023.
It was directed by John Contini.

Woman: Jane Paradise
Man: Reginald Pierre

(left to right) Jane Paradise, Reginald Pierre
Photo: STLAS

LIGHTS UP ON TWO CHAIRS. COMFORTABLE IN THE WAY THAT THEY ARE AT A THEATER OR A CINEMA. NEXT TO EACH OTHER. A MAN IS SEATED IN ONE. MIDDLE-AGED. BLACK. HE IS GLANCING AT THE PLAYBILL IN HIS HANDS AND LOOKING AROUND THE AUDITORIUM (OUT TO THE AUDIENCE). HE HAS A COAT ON HIS LAP. AFTER A FEW BEATS A WOMAN ENTERS, CHECKING HER TICKET, THEN SITS NEXT TO HIM. ABOUT THE SAME AGE. WHITE. SHE IS CARRYING A NUMBER OF BAGS (PURSE, TOTE, ETC.) AND SHE TAKES HER TIME REMOVING THEM AND ARRANGING THEM, ALONG WITH HER COAT. AFTER A MOMENT SHE IS SEATED AND GLANCES OVER AT THE MAN NEXT TO HER, WHO HAS BEEN WATCHING HER THE WHOLE TIME. SHE SMILES, THEN BEGINS DIGGING THROUGH HER PURSE. HE LOOKS AWAY AND CHECKS THE TIME. GLANCES AT HER AGAIN THEN GOES BACK TO THE PLAYBILL IN HIS HANDS. SHE FINDS SOME GUM AND OPENS A PIECE. THE MAN LOOKS OVER AT HER AND SHE OFFERS THE PACK. HE SHAKES HIS HEAD 'NO' AS HE GOES BACK TO READING. SHE POPS THE GUM IN HER MOUTH AND STARTS CHEWING. CHECKS HER OWN TIME AND THEN SITS AND WAITS. THE MAN FINISHES WITH THE PLAYBILL AND PLACES IT ON HIS COAT. THE WOMAN LOOKS AT HIM AND THEN NUDGES HIM WITH AN ELBOW. HE TURNS TO HER AS SHE LEANS OVER AND WHISPERS:

WOMAN ...do you mind?

MAN What's that?

WOMAN (POINTING) Can I look at yours? (HE LOOKS AT HER FOR A BEAT, THEN AT HIS PLAYBILL, WITHOUT SAYING ANYTHING) No big deal, I just didn't get one on the way in, they didn't give me one, so I thought if you were done, then I could just-- (SHE'S STARTING TO GET A VIBE). You know what? Not a problem...I can just...go...

MAN Here. (HE HANDS IT OVER WITHOUT LOOKING AT HER AND CHECKS THE TIME AGAIN)

WOMAN I don't have to if it bothers you.

MAN No, go ahead.

WOMAN You sure?

MAN Yes.

WOMAN You sure sure?

MAN ....

WOMAN Thanks. (BEAT) Some people save 'em and so, you know, they don't want any fingerprints on 'em or whatever and I get that, I respect it, but I usually just check out the cast and the articles and then, you know... (GESTURES) Toss it under my seat on the way out, so...

MAN I'll take mine back when you finish with it.

WOMAN Cool. No problem. Thanks. (SILENCE AS SHE LEAFS THROUGH IT, STOPPING AT DIFFERENT SPOTS AND READING. FINALLY SHE FINDS AN IN- SERT IN THE PLAYBILL AND READS IT. LOOKS OVER AT THE MAN AND THEIR EYES MEET) Is this why you're being a little huffy with me...because of this?

MAN Excuse me?

SHE SHOWS HIM THE SLIP OF PAPER BUT HE DOESN'T READ IT AS HE MAIN- TAINS EYE CONTACT WITH HER.

WOMAN Is this the problem?

MAN I don't have a problem...do you have a problem?

WOMAN Nope.

MAN Ok, then...

WOMAN I just thought that maybe...

MAN (CURTLY) You thought wrong.

WOMAN Alright, good.

MAN I'm just waiting for the show to get started, that's all...

WOMAN Fine.

MAN I don't have any problem...so...

WOMAN I get it, ok, you don't have a problem. (BEAT) You got no problem.

MAN That's right.

WOMAN Fair enough. My mistake.

MAN Good.

WOMAN Yep. Great.

MAN Ok then...

WOMAN Here.

SHE SLIPS THE PIECE OF PAPER BACK INSIDE THE PLAYBILL AND GIVES IT TO THE MAN. TURNS BACK IN HER OWN SEAT.
 I can sit somewhere else...

MAN No, you can't.

WOMAN Ummmm....

MAN Look around. It's sold out.

WOMAN Oh, yeah...you're right...

MAN I know I am. It's packed. There's no other seat available for you.

WOMAN Ok, well, then...

MAN You took the last one.

WOMAN Well, that's not...exactly...

MAN Took it from somebody else.

WOMAN Ummmmm...

MAN Didn't you?

WOMAN Well...I mean...I booked a ticket, so, yeah, that takes one seat off the market from other people, but--

MAN And presumably you knew about this, right? (PULLS THE SLIP OUT OF THE PLAYBILL) Or are you gonna say you didn't know this was happening...? Are you gonna say that to my face?

WOMAN No.

MAN I didn't think so.

WOMAN   You didn't think what?

MAN   I didn't think that you didn't know about this...

WOMAN   Meaning...you thought that I knew.

MAN   Yes.

WOMAN   Ummmmm...yeah, I did...I saw it on the website when I booked but it's not...you know...it definitely said that I could still come tonight if I wanted to or needed to and I did, I needed to see this performance...tonight...so that's not...I'm not trying to rationalize this or to...you know...apologize...for...

MAN   ...ok...

WOMAN   I'm not, because I have nothing to apologize for...I appreciate what they're doing here, with the whole 'black out' thingie, but--actually I don't know if I do, 'appreciate' it, I mean, I don't know if I do--but I understand it, the idea of it and so, yeah, whatever, do that if you really need to...but I work and this was the only night that fit my schedule so I got a ticket for the show tonight and so that's why I'm here. (BEAT) Not to make trouble or anything like that. (BEAT) I am not making a statement by being here...I just needed tonight and I came and that's it. (SMILES) Not making a scene.

MAN   But...you kind of are, though...

WOMAN   Like...ok, yes, maybe it does do it simply by me being here but that's not my motive...this was not, like, a planned event. Yes, 'planned' as in my coming tonight but not in a political way...not in a cultural way...this is just me wanting to see a show that people have been talking about and me going 'hey, I can only see it on Friday' and so I checked it out and there was a single available and I took it.

MAN   And so then somebody else won't see it because of you.

WOMAN   Ummmmm...ok...yes...not tonight...but I'm sure that it's...

MAN   You stopped somebody else from the experience by taking that ticket... maybe the only chance they'd have, so, I think that is a statement.

WOMAN   Right...but then...so did you.

MAN   Excuse me?

WOMAN   You did the same thing.

MAN   Excuse me, but it's not the same...me being here's NOT the same thing.

WOMAN   How is it not the same thing?

MAN   Another black person might have had that seat if you'd just followed the instructions and bought your...

WOMAN   They were not instructions.

MAN   Ummmmm...yes, they were...

WOMAN   No...that's not true...

MAN   There was definitely instructions on what to do or not do on the...

WOMAN   No, no, hold on, no, hold it...lemme just get the...thingie...

THE MAN RELUCTANTLY STOPS WHILE THE WOMAN DIGS INSIDE HER BAG FOR HER PHONE. SHE PULLS IT OUT AND WORKS TO FIND SIGNAL. SHE FINALLY GETS SOME AND PUSHES SOME BUTTONS. FINDS WHAT SHE IS LOOKING FOR AND TURNS TO HIM. READING.
Ok. Good. Here. (READS) "While this performance has been arranged for black audience members specifically, no one is excluded from attending." (BEAT) So.

MAN   As I said...

WOMAN   What? You said that there was...

MAN   Instructions, yes, and there were. "This performance has been arranged for black audience members..."

WOMAN   Yes, ok, but so what, though? It was 'arranged' for you and not me, that's fine...look around you...pretty damned successful; I see three other white faces here, so, like, 97% effective in having the place to yourselves--so just look at the stage and don't look over at me and you'll have your big 'black night' and we'll both be happy. (BEAT) Ok? Does that really sound like such a hard thing to do...? Honestly...?

MAN   Let's just leave it alone and watch the show. Ok? I don't want to talk about it any more right now...

WOMAN   Ok, yeah, but you kinda did before, when I first sat down, with that look on your face...

MAN   I barely glanced at you.

WOMAN   No, that's...you had a look, don't say that you didn't...because...

MAN   I was surprised, that's all...

WOMAN   Mmmmmm-hmmmmm...

MAN   I was!

WOMAN   It looked like a little bit more than that to me...but...ok...

MAN   Well, I'm sorry, but that's all it was...'surprise'...I didn't expect you and that was all...

WOMAN   'Me' or someone like me? You mean a white person, right?

MAN   I'm not gonna do this right now...

WOMAN   I see. (BEAT) So you booked in for this specifically, is that right? For this special 'black night' and me showing up has kinda freaked you out...is that it...basically...?

MAN   That's right, and not 'freaked,' it didn't do that to me...it surprised me, that's all. It surprised me.

WOMAN   Because what...lemme guess...I bet I can get it almost word for word from what's on the website. (THINKS) Because you thought you'd be 'freed from the tyranny of the white gaze.'

MAN   ...

WOMAN   (LOOKING AT HER PHONE) I mean...I nailed it. See? (HOLDS UP HER CELL) Word for word. Like exactly word-for-word.

HE PRETENDS TO CLAP AND SHE PRETENDS TO BOW. ANOTHER MINUTE OR TWO OF SILENCE BETWEEN THEM BEFORE HE SAYS:

MAN And is that such a bad thing...? Looking forward to what was being offered to me?

WOMAN I dunno...is it?

MAN This is ridiculous!

SHE WAITS A MOMENT THEN CONTINUES, PRESSING HIM WITH:

WOMAN What about me...do they have a show for just women 'freed from the tyranny of the male gaze?' (BEAT) I don't think so and who knows, maybe I would've booked for that one if they did...

MAN I thought tonight was your only night.

WOMAN Ok, yes, good one. Touche.

MAN Isn't it, or was that a lie?

WOMAN No, it is, yeah, but...I'm...

MAN Look, you're just being confrontational now, so let's just...

WOMAN No, I'm not.

MAN Yes, you are.

WOMAN I am not. Seriously, I'm just asking you a question.

MAN What?

WOMAN Why is this so important to you? Hmmmm? (BEAT) Is this play only about race? Does it not have any other issues in it, is it not a story about a family, about two people who are married and have children, who are out of work? Are you married? I was. Do you have children? I do. (BEAT) Do you really think that all those things are gonna matter to you more than they will to me, that you can only enjoy them if you're surrounded by black people--whom you are not supposed to be talking to or looking at during the show, by the way-- you don't think that you and I can sit here next to each other and both enjoy the show equally (or almost as much)? We don't have to exchange another word if you don't want to but we can sit here and watch and ponder and it shouldn't matter who we are--man, woman, black, white--it's a play and it's entertainment and we don't need to put up more barriers than there already are out there, especially not in here...not in the theater...now everybody says this is supposed to be a safe space...some place where everyone gets to play and no one gets their feelings hurt; why does theater need to be safe? Hmmmmm? Fine, what-ever, yes, you shouldn't get killed there or die in a fire, but safe? Says who...? I think they should be dangerous places, spaces where anything can and should be said, or seen, or questioned. This is the place to do all that--inside these four walls--where we can watch and learn and grow. This, right here, is where any subject can be brought up and discussed, not just the ones you like or I like... but everything. Anything that people want to explore, as long as they do it well. That's my only criteria. Just-Do-It-Well. Otherwise, I've got no time for it. (BEAT) Whatever, I don't give a shit, not really, but that's just what I think. (BEAT) Sorry, I can talk a lot sometimes, but, hey, that's how I actually feel about all this...

THEY SIT QUIETLY FOR A MOMENT WITHOUT LOOKING AT EACH OTHER. AFTER A WHILE, THE MAN SPEAKS WITHOUT TURNING HIS HEAD:

MAN   It's meant to be a positive thing.

WOMAN   *Sorry?*

MAN   Tonight...this...it's supposed to be positive...community building and therapeutic...that's the idea, anyway. A night for 'black pain,' because you know what? There has been a LOT of that lately--there always is--but it's been pretty damn shitty the last little bit, what with the Supreme Court and all that crap, police violence, plus my own family stuff...so I guess, yeah, I booked this thing looking for a bit of comfort, ok? That's all...just thought I'd come here tonight and do this, hang with folks and do...whatever.... (BEAT) But I guess it ain't no big thing if you REALLY gotta interrupt all that due to your 'schedule' and whatnot...

WOMAN   Yeah, and that's great if you can do that...

MAN   ...

WOMAN   People coming to the theater, I'm all for it, believe me...I work in a theater so I want nothing more than audiences for everybody...

MAN Same for me. I want that, too.

WOMAN Then we agree.

MAN But...?

WOMAN No 'but.'

MAN Sounded like you had a 'but' coming but maybe not...

WOMAN No...not really...I just...

MAN 'But.'

WOMAN Ok, yeah...BUT...not like this. Not this way. (BEAT) This is divisive. It's wrong...it's ghetto-izing.

MAN 'Ghetto-izing?' Please. It's one night...that's all...one out of 36...so why can't we just do this small but important thing on one night out of the entire run of this play? Hmmmm? Something just for us? For MY people...for MY audience?

WOMAN You can...you obviously can and you are...but why does it always have to be about us and them? Why can't I also come and it doesn't have to set us back five hundred years, just because tonight fits into my very hectic life schedule. You may be black but I have *kids*; maybe they should have a mother's night! Now there's somebody who needs a safe space! (LOOKS AROUND) They're late... they must be holding the curtain for...something...or...

MAN You maybe.

WOMAN Ha! Yeah, no doubt...

MAN Could be.

WOMAN (POINTING) White lady! Stop the presses!

MAN May-be...

WOMAN I kinda doubt it, though.

MAN You never know.

WOMAN   Yeah, maybe I'll have to go see one of the 'in-house counselors' out in the lobby after...because I've been so triggered by this experience... (LAUGHS) Can you believe that shit? God, that makes me laugh...

MAN   Jesus Christ, you're gonna make fun of that now, too...?

WOMAN   Kinda, yeah.

MAN   Wow, you're something...

WOMAN   Come on...counselors in the lobby for *a play*? That's bullshit...

MAN   To you, maybe...

WOMAN   Please. (BEAT) It's a stunt.

MAN   Ok, because you know everything...

WOMAN   No, because I work at a theater and I know a PR trick when I see one...

MAN   My God, you are cynical...

WOMAN   A little bit, maybe, but not that much. I'm a realist, that's all...

MAN   That's a nice name for what you are.

WOMAN   Ooooohhhh...no more Mr. Nice Guy, huh?

MAN   Nope!

WOMAN   Ha! Good! I prefer the truth...

MAN   Oh, no, you don't, you don't want the real truth...

WOMAN   Yes, I do...go ahead...

MAN   No, seriously, we can go back and forth on this shit all night, but let's be honest here...you do not actually wanna know what I think about you showing up here tonight, on this one particular night... (BEAT) I know you don't.

WOMAN   Says you.

MAN   Ok, I think it sucks. (BEAT) There.

WOMAN ...

MAN Told you you wouldn't like it...

WOMAN No, that's ok, if that's you being honest then that's ok with me. You think it's wrong, me being here...

MAN I do. I think it's self-serving and a little bit...mean...

WOMAN Why, because I'm white or...because I didn't follow the rules? (BEAT) Which bothers you the most?

MAN Both. Probably.

WOMAN So if I was Asian it'd be better?

MAN Oh-my-God.

WOMAN I'm just asking!

MAN So...then...yes, it would be...

WOMAN Wow. Ok. Actual honesty.

MAN Not perfect but better and you know why...I know I don't have to tell you why...

WOMAN Because in the history of the world Asian people have never killed or raped or enslaved anybody...right?

MAN ...no...

WOMAN Ok...then...why...?

SHE WAITS FOR HIM TO SPEAK BUT HER EYE CATCHES SOMEONE MOVING DOWN THE AISLE NEAR THEM (UNSEEN).
An usher is going backstage...

MAN Something's up...

WOMAN Maybe they just spotted me...

MAN Maybe so...

WOMAN   Ha! (BEAT) You're not gonna make me feel bad about this...I promise.

MAN   I know I'm not...

WOMAN   But you're gonna try anyway...

MAN   Maybe...

WOMAN   That's crazy! (BEAT) Who cares? No, but, like, seriously, who the hell actually cares about me? Right...? Just try and enjoy the show, connect with it no matter who is sitting here next to you...you're supposed to be looking in that direction, not at me...! (BEAT) It's ridiculous, really, the whole damn concept of these things, created by some moron who's just trying to get noticed and stir up trouble, a needy little 'look at me' asshole.

MAN   Says the white lady...

WOMAN   Says the person who probably makes a LOT less at her job than you do, ok, but doesn't need a special slot at the theater for 'poor people' to make her feel *safe*...

MAN   Interesting politics.

WOMAN   Yeah, reality's a bitch, isn't it? Sorry...

THE MAN IS ABOUT TO SAY SOMETHING BUT CATCHES HIMSELF. THEN:

MAN   You know what, can you just leave me alone, please? Can we stop talking and just let me sit here and get ready for the performance...? Would that be okay with you...?

WOMAN   Sure...I mean...I'd much rather ask you deeply personal questions to shame you about your heritage and your workplace and understand why you're so damn touchy but yes, we can just wait quietly for the show to begin if you want to... (BEAT) I'm kidding. (ZIPS HER LIPS) Mum's the word.

MAN   Thank you.

WOMAN   Welcome. (BEAT) You know they did a thing like this in New York once...in Brooklyn, maybe...for a movie, it was WONDER WOMAN, I think, they did 'female only' screenings a few times so that women could go to see the film 'safely' with other women and/or 'female identifying' people, and so they did that...the theater did, I think, not the company releasing the film, which was SONY, and they don't give a shit, so long as lots and lots and lots of people went to see it...anyway, that happened in New York. (BEAT) Not the second film, not the one that takes place in the 80s, this was for the first one. The good one.

MAN Huh.

WOMAN Yeah.

MAN And did you go...?

WOMAN God no! We were living there at the time, in Queens, actually, not in Brooklyn, but no...I mean, think about it, it sounded so fucking stupid...a screening of WONDER WOMAN that was 'female friendly.' What am I, five years old? It's the movies! Ooh, daddy, someone is staring at me while I watch these huge fucking Amazon ladies kick the living shit out of every man for a hundred miles around...I mean, come on...grow the hell up! I've never felt nervous at the movies, not once in my life--on my way there, yes, on the sidewalk after, or at some guy's house on a date I'm with--but never while I was watching the actual movie. Not ever. (BEAT) Anyway, I saw it at my local AMC with my kids, like everybody else.

MAN Like most everybody else.

WOMAN I stand corrected. Yes. 'Most.'

MAN Yeah, well, I still don't think that's quite the same thing...

WOMAN It isn't?

MAN As this? No...not exactly...

WOMAN Because...?

MAN Look...I really don't wanna get into it with you...I don't know you and I'm just trying to see a show and relax, so let's not...

WOMAN Then fine. Stop talking to me and wait for the show to start and we can drop the subject...

MAN   I'm not talking to you.

WOMAN   You have been. A lot.

MAN   And you've been talking at me...

WOMAN   Didn't say I wasn't.

MAN   So...then...

WOMAN   What?

MAN   Just...whatever! Leave me be!

SHE MIMES BEING CAREFUL AND SITS BACK IN HER SEAT. WAITING. THE MAN SHAKES HIS HEAD AND MUTTERS SOMETHING TO HIMSELF.

WOMAN   What's that...?

MAN   Nothing.

WOMAN   Oh, ok.

MAN   ...

WOMAN   You sure?

MAN   Yes. Why?

WOMAN   Just because it sounded like you did it just loud enough for me to hear you but not understand it so I'd have to ask you what you said. That's why.

MAN   It was nothing.

WOMAN   Ok.

MAN   Honestly...I just said...'people.'

WOMAN   Ahhh.

MAN   That's all.

WOMAN   You mean 'white people.'

MAN   That's not what I said...

WOMAN   Sure, I know, but…that's who you mean. (BEAT) Me. Us. White folks.

MAN   I just don't understand you, that's all.

WOMAN   And I don't understand you and that is fine with me…we don't have to. Ever. Why do we think that it's SO important to, like, communicate and be understood and all that shit…when we can very easily just get on with it by doing our own thing and not really understanding each other and that's just fine…you do you and I'll do me and we don't need to be friends. (BEAT) I came to this, whatever, your precious little…'black night'…and it shouldn't matter to you if I'm here or not, that's what I think…my actions don't matter in the end. At all.

MAN   'Black-out night.' 'Black-out.'

WOMAN   Whatever!

MAN   There's a difference…ok?

WOMAN   Which would be what…?

MAN   Just…it's semantics…! (BEAT) This is meant to be a celebration, ok, a gathering and a kind of…whatever…like, a homecoming for me and people like me…but that just bugs the living shit outta you, doesn't it? Hmmmm?

WOMAN   No, it doesn't. (BEAT) My God, you are just SO ready to be offended!

MAN   And you are SO ready to offend!

WOMAN   Maybe because you need to lighten up about yourself a little bit…

MAN   Who does?

WOMAN   You do…people like you…

MAN   'Black people,' you mean.

WOMAN   No, 'easily offended' people, I mean.

MAN   Jesus, you have no understanding of things and how they…*of history*…or anything…do you?

WOMAN   Well, that's actually not true…

MAN   Really?

WOMAN   Yeah, that's not true at all.

MAN   Prove it.

WOMAN   'Prove it?' Ok...wow...ummmmmm...you like the idea of tonight with no real reason why...if I pressed you on it--and I'm not going to--but you want it because it feels good...it feels like you're getting something that other people aren't getting--namely, white people--and that's enough of a reason for you, which I think is kind of childish and reactionary and just...not...necessary, especially in a theater during a show that has an almost entirely black creative team and an all-black cast and an audience, tonight, at least, that is nearly completely black. But if we really kept arguing about it, if we did, at some point you'd hit me with 1619 and red-lining and oppression and all this shit that just doesn't really matter any more...stuff that we could put behind us if you would just do that... just say it's the past, that people suck and a lot of bad stuff that was really really wrong happened historically but it's done now and you personally are fine and it's time to move the fuck on...but you can't...can you? No, you can't, and I'm not entirely sure you want to, either, because it's your thing now and it's who you are and it defines you and it's kind of this...badge of honor or something at this point, it's your burden...which is fair, maybe, it's terrible and you deserve lots of things--sympathy and 'I'm sorry' and all kinds of shit, I'm SO fine with that-- but not this. Not here. The theater is a wonderful place, it's a magical space and we should come here to be together...not to grow further apart. (BEAT) Blackout Nights. I mean, come on! (BEAT) You're just making yourselves look bad. I'm... serious...it's silly, doing stupid shit like this...you look foolish. (BEAT) That's how I feel about it, anyway. (BEAT) So.

MAN   That is...completely and utterly offensive...

WOMAN   Ok...but...

MAN   Beyond...it's beyond offensive. (BEAT) If you were a man I'd hit you right in the fucking face...

WOMAN   But you haven't said I'm wrong yet...

MAN Of course you are!

WOMAN Of course I am…and if this was a 'white out' night designed so a white audience could have a….

MAN No, no, no…there is no outrage equivalency here, forget that…

WOMAN No, I'm just saying…

MAN There isn't! Forget about it! It doesn't exist, so just don't…!

WOMAN That's not what I'm saying, I'm just asking IF there was a show set aside one night for 'us' to enjoy without having to suffer a black gaze or however you'd call it…what about that? Would that be alright? (BEAT) Of course it wouldn't! Of course not…!

MAN "You mean, 'any other night of the week…?'"

WOMAN Ha! Really, you think so…?

MAN At most theaters, yes.

WOMAN But we're talking about this one…about this show. (BEAT) Who's been the primary audience for this show so far, do you think? I wonder…

MAN I mean…

WOMAN Actually that's not true, because I know someone who works here and we talk all the time and so I know the answer already…over the run thus far the audience has been 85% black and 15% whoever else, so, you know, I think you're wrong about it…this show, at least…so I hope that makes you feel a little bit more 'safe' tonight.

MAN Is that right?

WOMAN It is, actually…yes.

MAN Huh.

WOMAN It's an actual fact.

THE MAN NODS AT THIS, TAKING IN THE INFORMATION. AFTER A BEAT HE

TURNS AND SPEAKS QUIETLY TO THE WOMAN:

MAN Well, here's another fact for you: my grandfather went to the movies when he was a kid...saved his pennies to go all week and on Saturdays he and his brothers would go to the movie house in the next town over--a five mile walk in both directions--he'd treat himself to a movie once or twice a month. (BEAT) This was in a place called Durham, North Carolina. At the Carolina Theater and it was a 97 step climb they had to do, up to the balcony where they were allowed to sit. Up in the Buzzard's Roost. The Peanut Gallery. (BEAT) This one time, his little brother was hanging over the edge and looking down--do you hear what I'm saying to you?--he's just a tiny little fella and he decides to get outta his chair and LOOK over the edge at all of those white boys and girls down there with their families, enjoying that air conditioning...and...some kid complained to his mommy or daddy about that 'dirty little nigger boy' staring down at them and so this manager came upstairs, sweating like a fucking pig from climbing all those stairs and hopping mad, and he dragged that eight year-old boy back down those stairs, those 97 steps, and he and another man who worked there beat him almost to death...beat the living shit outta him...until he was knocked out and unconscious and couldn't walk if he had to...but his three brothers had to somehow get him back home those five miles...they stole a wheelbarrow, a thing that could've got them shot dead back then--or today--and so those three young men took turns pushing him home in the bed of that rusty ol' contraption. (BEAT) So yeah...feeling 'safe' is A-OK by me. It is quite alright.

THE MAN FINISHES AND TURNS AWAY FROM HER, BACK TO HIS PLAYBILL. QUICKLY LEAFS THROUGH IT, THEN CHECKS THE TIME.

WOMAN Ok. (BEAT) That's awful.

THE WOMAN STARES AT THE STAGE IN FRONT OF HER. WAITS FOR THE SHOW TO BEGIN BUT IT DOESN'T. AFTER A MINUTE, SHE SAYS:
Probably about that same time...over in Europe...my grandmother was pulled out of a ballet performance she attended with her mother and was rounded up and sent to a camp in Poland. Never saw her family again, just her mother, at least up until the train stopped and the men with dogs herded them off the car they were in, and then her mother was gone as well. Just gone. (BEAT) Somehow my grandmother...she made it, don't ask me how, but she did, the rest of her family

was wiped out...wiped off the face of the earth but not her. She lived. She lived a very long life and you know what? She went to the ballet every season for the rest of her days...and I went with her for years and years and years, when I was younger and she never, not once, asked for an all-female audience or an all-Jewish audience or anything like that...my grandma sat next to men and women, bad people and German people and she watched those shows and she loved all the dance and the costumes and the music and that was that. (BEAT) Life is what you make of it, you know? That's what she thought and she told me that, over and over and over again...and that is what I believe as well. (POINTS AT THE STAGE) Just watch the show, don't worry about me and I won't worry about you and ya know what? We are gonna be just fine...both of us. (BEAT) I know we will. (THE MAN LOOKS AT HER BUT SAYS NOTHING. FINALLY HE SHAKES HIS HEAD AND TURNS BACK TOWARD THE STAGE) I *know* it.

MAN   You don't want this to be a contest, I promise you don't...

WOMAN   What's that?

MAN   Pain...and hate...and suffering...

WOMAN   You're right, I don't...and it's not...it's not and it never should be.

MAN   But if it was...

WOMAN   You'd lose.

HE TURNS QUICKLY AND LOOKS AT HER, CATCHING HIMSELF BEFORE HE SAYS SOMETHING STUPID. SHE SMILES AT HIM DISARMINGLY.
And so would I. We both would. (BEAT) Because there is always a story that's worse than ours somewhere out there...ALWAYS. Sadder than ours, more devastating than ours. Always always always. It's the way of the world...

HE LOOKS AWAY. WHETHER OR NOT HE AGREES WITH HER HE IS DONE TALK -ING ABOUT IT AND SO HE SITS AND WAITS.
I'm sorry for ruining your evening.

MAN   You didn't.

WOMAN   Yeah? You sure about that?

MAN You don't have that power.

WOMAN Good. I'm glad I don't.

MAN ...

WOMAN I hope no one in your life ever does...that's my wish for you.

MAN And...I hope your work schedule lightens up soon...that's my wish for you.

WOMAN Ha! I could take that a number of ways.

MAN Yes, you could.

WOMAN Ok.

MAN Ok then.

WOMAN Thanks.

MAN You're welcome.

WOMAN Enjoy the show.

MAN (AFTER A MOMENT) You, too.

THEY GLANCE AT EACH OTHER AND THEN GATHER THEMSELVES AS THE LIGHTS BEGIN TO GO DOWN. HE REACHES FOR HIS PLAYBILL AND SLIDES IT OVER TO HER. SHE SEES THIS AND, SURPRISED BY THE GESTURE, TAKES IT.

WOMAN (WHISPERING) And if you need to talk to somebody afterwards... I'll be here if you need me...out in the lobby. (BEAT) Just saying.

FOR THE FIRST TIME, THE MAN SMILES AT THIS AND NODS.

MAN Ha! I might take you up on that.

WOMAN I dare you to.

MAN I just might.

WOMAN ...

MAN You never know.

WOMAN No. You never do.

SHE IS ABOUT TO SPEAK AGAIN BUT MUSIC UP AND LIGHTS DOWN. THE SHOW HAS FINALLY BEGUN AND THE MAN AND THE WOMAN QUICKLY GET LOST IN THE PLAY IN FRONT OF THEM. THEY SMILE AT DIFFERENT TIMES, LAUGH AT DIFFERENT THINGS, BUT THEY ARE BOTH HAPPY AND ENGAGED AND ENTER-TAINED. WATCHING.